STRAIGHT AS AN ARROW

STRAIGHT AS AN ARROW

CELESTINE SIBLEY

HarperCollins*Publishers*

13 1 4 8 3 1 5

HarperCollins books may be purchased for educational, business, or sales promotional use. For information, please call or
write: Special Markets Department, HarperCollins Publishers,
Inc., 10 East 53rd Street, New York, NY 10022.

FIRST EDITION

Designed by Alma Hochhauser Orenstein

Library of Congress Cataloging-in-Publication Data

Sibley, Celestine.
    Straight as an arrow / Celestine Sibley.—1st ed.
        p.   cm.
    ISBN 0-06-016305-4 (cloth)
    I. Title.
PS3569. I526S7   1992
813'.54—dc20   91-58337

92 93 94 95 96 ❖/RRD 10 9 8 7 6 5 4 3 2 1

For Helen Pratt, stellar agent and patient friend

ACKNOWLEDGMENTS

With gratitude for their expertise and generous help to:

Dr. Tully Blalock, who knows about bullet wounds and blood. Dr. Ivan Backerman, physician and flyer, and Susie, his wife and copilot, who told me about her old club the Ninety-Nines, and to both of them for many island trips in their plane. My coworker, Forrest Rogers, flyer and son of Rock Rogers, who gave me my first flying lesson. For Sibley Fleming, who taught me about gambling. For my grandson Charles Fleming, called Bird, and his mentor at Georgia State University Library, Mrs. Elizabeth Cooksey, who knows about Indians and Indian mounds. And finally for the friends, not a murderer among them, on my own favorite Gulf island, called Dog.

1

Kate Mulcay was loyal to Atlanta weather. She told everybody it was the most exciting, most benevolent weather in the country, one lovely season ripening and mellowing into the next with sumptuous variety. You never weary of Atlanta weather, she assured newcomers and visitors and random acquaintances in far places, because whatever it is, it never lasts more than a swift and ephemeral day or two.

Of course, there was the summer of the heat wave and extended drought, but that was truly unusual. One winter an ice storm strung utility wires and tree branches with crystal and spread a glittering counterpane of snow over streets and the countryside, but that was a six-day wonder and the locals loved it. Rain, sleet, and gray wintry days came, as in other less fortunate climes, and then departed with gracious celerity.

Oh, Kate would never allow a word said against Atlanta weather—until January 1991, when it turned faithless. She had held that Shakespeare, writing of

Cleopatra, for whom custom never staled her famous "infinite variety," could well have known Atlanta weather. But then, Cleo had been faithless, too.

Slogging home from her morning walk, a daily effort to mortify the flesh and maybe lose some of it, she counted up the days of leaden skies and cold unrelenting rain, which even now drove needles into the shoulders of her running suit and down her collar. Monday had been dishwater gray, Tuesday foggy, Wednesday had a nasty biting wind, and here it was Thursday and raining again, muckily, mercilessly.

Her dirt road, a usually captivating thoroughfare of a couple of miles worn through the woods a hundred years ago by mules and oxen pulling farm wagons to the old country store up on the highway, was a mud puddle. An old crabapple tree by a long since abandoned house site would be a tower of pink blooms and heavenly fragrance in another month or two. Now it was a skeleton, green-lichened and sinister. Fog swaddled the woods at the edge of the abandoned fields. The field larks, which normally noted her passage with flutelike whistles, were silent. Even her dog, Pepper, who usually ran ahead of her to sniff out earth fragrances and hold at bay any highwaymen who dared venture down her road, trudged dully in her footsteps, yawning now and then to let her know he'd rather be on his old Army blanket on the floor by the kitchen door.

Me, too, Kate silently acknowledged his unspoken wish. *Why didn't I stay in bed?* She had the rest of the week and the weekend off from her job as a reporter-columnist for the *Atlanta Searchlight*, time she fully intended to spend ordering and starting seeds for her garden and transplanting small trees and shrubs from the woods to the thicket she was gradually building between her log cabin and the road. Instead, the earth was too cold and soggy for digging, and the bright opulence of bloom promised by the seed catalogs seemed a cruel fantasy in this weather.

Kate stamped up the steps of the back porch of her little cabin, pausing to divest herself of muddy boots and leaving them by the door.

The phone was ringing off the kitchen wall.

There was trouble on the line and for a few seconds all Kate could hear was a woman's faint voice crying "Kate! Kate!" and then a mechanical keening. She started to hang up to give the caller a chance to dial again, and then she recognized the imperious voice of Nora Noble promising to have the entire telephone system put out of business if it did not allow her to speak to Kate Mulcay up north of Atlanta, Georgia, immediately.

"It's an emergency!" she finished in a tone the telephone system seemed to choke on but missed swallowing.

"Nora!" cried Kate. "You've got me! What's the emergency? I'm listening. What's up?"

"Oh, Kate," said Nora, sighing. "I'm not sure it's an emergency. I just said that. But then ..." she paused, "it might be. Something funny is happening here on the island. I want you to get on down here."

Kate looked around the old pine walls of her kitchen, searching for an excuse. She loved Ila Island—

so much that she had persuaded her husband Benjy to buy a lot and build a little vacation house there. Now Benjy was dead and she rented out the cottage or lent it to friends, and she wasn't sure she would ever want to go there again. The months they had worked together building a place on the beach were among the happiest of their twenty-year marriage. She had reminders enough here in this old log cabin they had found and restored together, but you have to be somewhere, she thought resignedly, and she had somehow hacked out a kind of acceptance here. By immersing herself in work at the newspaper and spending a lot of time on her knees in the yard, she ached with loneliness intermittently, but she had not dissolved under the bitter wave of grief.

"Kate! Kate!" Nora was calling again. "Are you coming? Answer me! It's urgent!"

"Oh, Nora, I don't think I can—" Kate began, but Nora interrupted.

"Kate, people are dying!"

Kate knew several old friends on the island had died in the last year or so. One elderly neighbor she and Benjy had loved died of cancer almost the same month Benjy had died. A couple who ran the only semi-commercial establishment on the island—an almost-convenience store called the Fo'castle, where beer and Cokes and cigarettes and an occasional bag of ice or loaf of bread could be bought—had suffered heart attacks and died within weeks of each other. A September storm, as if tidying up memories and loss, had swept away the Fo'castle a month after their deaths.

"I know, Nora," Kate murmured, "and it makes me sad, but I don't know what I can do."

"You can find the killer, Kate!" cried Nora. "Aren't you good at detecting? Don't you work with the police all the time? Well, you better get down here. I think it's murder!"

Before Kate could demur again, the line went dead and she was left standing there in her wet sock feet, amused and not believing but oddly disturbed in spite of herself. Nora Noble was no crackpot. It was true she read a lot of murder mysteries. That was basic fare on the island in wintertime. The few people who remained there when the hurricanes came and left passed murder mysteries back and forth as if they were throwing life preservers to one another.

Nora and her husband, Philip, were the most seasoned islanders among a handful of year-round settlers on Ila. They subscribed to book clubs, making themselves very popular between November and April. After that the population burgeoned. Easter holidays brought families back with their children. College students rented cottages for noisy house parties. Even settled settlers like Kate mended old bathing suits and rummaged for faded beach towels and thought wistfully of the opalescent tides and the shell-littered white beaches of the Gulf of Mexico.

Even now, standing by the kitchen window and listening to the furnace making guttural sounds in the corner back of the cookbook shelf, she knew she should call the propane gas company for a refill of the big tank in the yard and prepare for bad weather. But her mind went to blue water and sand dunes snowy against cedar and pine, and, best of all, sunshine. She might call Nora back and make sure that it was summertime on Ila.

But she knew Nora had called from a pay station outside the only grocery store in Simolona, the little mainland town nearest Ila, and she had probably already crossed the street to the marina and cranked up for the trip back across the sound.

Kate packed sweaters and wool pants instead of bathing suits and beach towels and searched the pantry for staples to take to Ila. She hadn't been there in so many months that her mental list of what was there and what was needed was already shattered. She grabbed a bag of French roast coffee, a brand she had taken up lately, deciding that milder brews did nothing for her. Other supplies she could pick up at the Simolona store—matches and dog food and milk and bread and eggs and sandwich makings. If she stayed only a weekend, she could make do with very little.

Years ago in a small town in south Georgia, where she had found lodging in an old country hotel around midnight, after a day of trudging through swamps looking for the burned bones of a murder victim, she had learned that you can make do with a jar of peanut butter. There had been no restaurants open, no fast food places. A filling station with a small shelf of groceries had sold her a jar of peanut butter, which, with a plastic spoon, provided day's-end nourishment. It was not her favorite fare, but it effectively staved off hunger for hours, sometimes for days. She seldom traveled without it, although nowadays there were all-night fast food

places open along most highways. She checked her K
ration as she let Pepper in the backseat of her car. Only
half a jar of ancient oily peanut butter. She threw it in
the garbage and drove down through the woods to alert
her neighbor, Miss Willie Wilcox, that she was going to
be away and to ask her to feed Sugar, the cat. It wasn't
really necessary. Sugar was already curled up on a cushion in front of Miss Willie's fireplace. That cat, like the
weather, was faithless, Kate decided, giving him a
farewell pat and hugging Miss Willie. Pepper would
grieve if she left him, but Sugar, monumentally self-
reliant, would simply find another cushion, another
saucer of milk.

On the off chance that she would be gone longer
than the weekend and that she might need it, Kate
stopped at the newspaper office to pick up a portable
computer and to tell her boss, City Editor Shell Shelnutt, that she was going. There was no point in giving
him addresses or telephone numbers. Mail to the island
was delivered only once a week—Wednesdays, as Kate
remembered—and there were no telephones. The ones
at the marina and at the on-shore home of the ferryboat
captain, who made the run to the island on weekends
only, were strictly emergency numbers. Messages, if
important, could be relayed by VHF radio, but they
were a lot of trouble to the recipient relayer and often
radios were tied up with the salty talk of the Marine
Patrol, the Coast Guard, and shrimpers. Kate had a VHF
Benjy had insisted on installing, but she never had been
sure how to operate it, and on the rare occasions when
she had tried, she felt self-consciously certain that her

message wasn't important enough for the airwaves. You couldn't really tie up the air with a call to your husband across the sound to be sure and bring salt or soap powder when he came.

Unlike the rest of the barrier islands that lay parallel to the Florida coast, Ila was a slender island thrusting out into the gulf like an arrow shot from the one-time Seminole Indian village, Simolona. The end closest to the shore, half a dozen miles from the mouth of the Simolona River, did from a distance look like the feathered stock of an arrow with its growth of pines and oaks and low-growing beach shrubs and little settlement of houses. Miles out into the gulf, it narrowed into a glistening ridge of white sand, connecting eventually with a high atoll so shaped that it was called the "arrowhead."

The rain fogged the windshield and the sound of the wipers was so soporific Kate feared she would go to sleep on I-75, most super of superhighways. She tried to focus her mind on the problems on Ila Island. If she hadn't known Nora Noble to be a steady, intelligent, long-headed woman, she would discount the urgency of her call. Why would anybody murder anybody on Ila, the last of the totally country barrier islands along the Gulf of Mexico coastline? Ambition and greed didn't afflict the islanders she knew. Some were affluent, but they were quiet unostentatious people, certainly not the kind to bring money or jewels or even a decent car to the island. Sand and salt air took a toll on metals on the island, and the latest car soon wore fenders that looked like rusty fringe, with engines and batteries that lapsed into monumental lethargy after a year or two.

Kate smiled to herself, remembering Benjy's aunt who had visited them at the beach a few times before she said apologetically, "Why would people on an island as pretty as this one have an old car graveyard right at the mouth of their harbor?"

Kate and Benjy had looked at one another and burst out laughing.

"That's not an old car graveyard," Benjy had said. "Those are the cars we travel in and they are parked in front of the yacht club."

And it was true that most of the people, who left their island vehicles when they boarded the ferry or their personal boats for the shore, parked them under the trees in close proximity to the little clapboard building which was labeled the Ila Yacht Club. She and Benjy had not joined the yacht club. Their little boat, far from being a yacht, seldom ran, and they felt they had no time or taste for clubby activities, although they knew and liked all the members and enjoyed the few parties to which they had been invited.

Their car would be there in the lineup next to the yacht club waiting for her, Kate thought worriedly, hoping it would run. Years ago the island had had a ferry which brought cars over from the mainland, but now they were down to a small passenger craft, and the only way to get a car over the sound was to hire a big work boat, a retired Army landing craft, which charged $250 a trip. That seemed immoderate expenditure to Kate for a vehicle which cost them only $75. Some friends of Benjy's father had sold them the car when they packed up to move to a retirement home. For a brief time it enjoyed celebrity on the island because it had lights and brakes and windshield wipers. And ran.

Thinking of the car, Kate was reminded to check the trunk of her land car before she got to Simolona to be sure she had the gas can to fill before she embarked for the island. She fished a notebook out of her bag and started a grocery list.

Time was when she and Benjy were new to the island, renting while they looked for a site for a house and then building it. She had expanded her kitchen skills, baking bread and making the seafood dishes he loved. Now ... peanut butter.

The rain quit about middle Georgia, but the fields where sweet potatoes and sugar cane and peanuts would grow were watery ditches. Spring planting was a month away and the tall skeletons of irrigation equipment, now lonely and useless, would be whirling away simulating rain for the thirsty fields. An island neighbor whose mainland business was manufacturing irrigating machinery designed to spew out treated and recycled sewage hit upon a great name, Benjy had always thought. He called it the Crapshooter.

Kate smiled, remembering, and turned off the expressway to the state road which would take her down to Tallahassee, the capital of Florida but still small and picturesque and live oak shaded, and past small towns with names like Omega, Enigma, Sopchoppy, and Panacea.

The grocery store in Simolona was preparing to close when Kate pulled up in front of it. She hurried in and filled her basket with minimum essentials, remembering to buy a jug of water for coffee. Island water was sulphur and all right for bathing and laundry and even mixed well enough with bourbon and scotch, but it retained the smell and, Kate suspected, the flavor of rotten eggs when you drank it plain or used it to make coffee. She picked up oranges and a yellow sheaf of bananas and lingered over the meat counter, trying to decide between steak and hamburger, finally taking both. And then just in case her island stay was longer than she anticipated, she asked the sleepy young man back of the counter about soup bones.

"We got them ugly oxtails," he said.

"Don't be flippant about oxtails," Kate scolded him, grinning broadly. "They make good soup. Lots of flavor."

"Help yourself," said the young man, delicately averting his face.

Kate inspected a package of chopped oxtail carefully, trying to decide why it was uglier than anything else that came off the cow. She would have no vegetables to go with it, except an onion and maybe a potato and a can of tomatoes, but she was almost certain there would be a jar of dried beans in the kitchen over the water. Nobody else, among renters and friends, liked them and cooked them as often as she did. She took the oxtails and headed for the checkout.

She had not begun to worry about how she would get to the island. The ferry would be running on Friday, but for tonight she might have to stay ashore in one of the clean, old-fashioned, family-run motels that hugged the bay shore. They were friendly and cheap and she had never minded the linoleum on the floor and the chenille bedspreads. They were faded but clean.

Nora Noble was waiting for her by the front door.

"Nora!" cried Kate, leaving her grocery cart and rushing to hug her. "Did you come to meet me?"

"What does it look like?" asked Nora with a smile that made her even teeth all the whiter against her island-browned face.

"How on earth did you know I'd be here?"

"I knew," said Nora. "I mentioned murder, didn't I?"

Kate laughed. "You have some atrocious idea that I am addicted to murders, don't you?"

Nora nodded and reached for the box of groceries. The clerks knew to pack boxes for the islanders because a trip over on a boat was nearly always a wet trip, dissolving brown paper bags and in time of rough wather pitching the lighter plastic bags overboard. Boxes were sturdy—and steady. All the islanders asked for them.

The Nobles' little launch waited by the dock at the marina, which had long since closed for the night. There was nobody around.

"Phil's not with you?" Kate said, missing Nora's husband.

Nora jumped on the bow and reached up for the box of groceries. She shook her head in its knitted Navy watch cap.

"Sick," she said. "I'll tell you about it."

"Seriously?" asked Kate. She was fond of lanky, sunbrowned Phil, who had retired early from a little air service he ran, which had included crop dusting and checking the big power line rights-of-way up in Georgia. He had heart trouble, but since coming to the island he claimed that peace and tranquility and benign weather had cured him. He had taken on several island jobs, mowing the little landing strip and keeping the dock in repair and collecting fees for the use of both. He kept his plane but seldom flew it. It wasn't much of an income, but Nora made a little cleaning houses and keeping an eye on them for summer people. They fished and shrimped and tonged oysters and ran a string of crab traps in season, and seemed content and comfortable.

Nora relieved Kate of Pepper's leash and guided him to his favorite spot as a sort of figurehead on the prow of the boat. She stowed away Kate's groceries and gas can and started the motor. They moved at a slow, no-wake pace out of the little harbor, past the lights of the Marine Patrol office and the dock, where a few shrimp boats were tied up.

The night was clear and a sky full of stars looked down on them. Kate thought about the little dark cottage that awaited her across the sound and wondered if she would be able to sleep there tonight or if the pain of missing Benjy would be too acute for endurance. Nora, always perceptive, sensed her uncertainty. She tilted her head and looked at the sky and quoted Carl Sandburg: "We may choose something like a star/ To stay our minds and be staid."

Kate wanted to reassure her. "I am staid, but I'm glad of the stars. Tell me about Phil. Is it his heart?"

They were passing the ferry dock and the no-wake piling. Nora eased the throttle forward, picking up speed, and fixed her eyes on the channel marker ahead.

"Somebody tried to kill him," she said.

"Who?" cried Kate. "How?"

"I don't know who," said Nora. "That's why I called you. But they did it with a snake."

"A snake!" Kate leaned forward and examined Nora's face in the light from the dash. It was damp from spray—and maybe tears—and older and more creased with wrinkles than Kate remembered.

Kate knew that the only thing under heaven that Philip Noble feared was snakes. His obsession was almost an island joke. There were snakes on the island, to be sure, but she had seen few. Once there was a cottonmouth moccasin floating languidly in the little creek near the airstrip, where she was blackberrying. And once when she and Benjy and the Nobles were picnicking a slim, fast black snake had raced over the dunes behind them, disappearing in a clump of yaupon.

She and Benjy had noted its passing casually and returned to their fried chicken and pimento cheese sandwiches. She looked up to see that Nora had taken hold of Philip's hand and was studying his face anxiously. He was very pale and the hand Nora held trembled.

"Hate those bastards," he said with a laugh when he could get his breath.

Benjy had looked at him reflectively and nodded.

"That old black snake wouldn't hurt you," he offered. "Good snake."

"I know," Phil said, "but I can't stand the sight of them, much less call on them for good deeds. It's the only reason I'd ever leave this island."

"Aw, don't say that," put in Kate. "Got to live and let live. They may help to keep down the coon and alligator populations." She was uncertain of her ecology, but she wanted to be reassuring.

Phil shook his head and gave up on the picnic food. He walked close to the tide line on the way back home, letting the little waves baste his ankles. Oddly enough, the other wildlife, feral cats and coons and alligators, and even the stingrays and sand sharks, didn't bother him. When they were fishing he even landed eels with equanimity. But snakes terrified him.

Now had he been bitten? She put the question to Nora over the sound of the motor and Nora shook her head.

"I'll tell you when we get there," she said.

Moments later she eased her little launch into its slip and threw a line to Kate, who climbed up on the pier and looped the line around a post.

Nora sat a moment looking at the night sky, her hands quiet on the steering wheel.

"Phil had a touch of flu," she said. "I made him stay in bed a day or two to get rid of it and he did seem better from the rest and all the liquids and stuff I gave him. I loaded his bedside table with some new murder mysteries and went down to the reef to look for oysters. You know where that is—in that little lagoon near the house. I'd been there maybe twenty or thirty minutes when I heard this awful screaming. Phil. I went running back and tore into the house and there on the little rug by our bed was the biggest rattlesnake you ever saw—not coiled, just waiting like. Motionless. I ran for the hoe and killed the snake and hauled him outside before I got to Phil. Kate, he was in agony. Pale green and gasping with the most awful pain in his chest. No doctor on the island, you know, and I was scared to try to get him to the dock and our boat. I called Tallahassee on the radio for the helicopter."

Kate waited, a sense of horror engulfing her.

"He's there now—out of intensive care but still weak."

"Oh, Nora," Kate said softly. "Oh, honey, how awful!"

"I think Phil is going to be all right," Nora said. "I'm going to bring him home tomorrow. I came back to get things ready here. The awful thing, Kate, is that somebody did it to him. And it could happen again. If it did, I think it would kill him."

Kate nodded. From what she knew of Philip Noble's obsession, she was practically sure he couldn't weather another such encounter.

"But who would do it?" Kate asked. "How do you haul a rattler around and how would they get it in your house without Phil hearing them or seeing them? He was awake, wasn't he?"

"I don't know," said Nora. "I suppose so. But it sure wasn't there when I left. I cleaned up before I went down to the oyster reef. Even ran the vacuum cleaner under the beds and into all the corners. And the door was closed tight. I did that to keep anybody from dropping in to visit Phil while he was resting. You know how it is on the island. People walk in if it's just the screened door, but they respect a tightly shut door."

"Oh, Nora, I don't see how I can help you with this. It's awful but I don't see—"

"That's not all," Nora said, pushing her watch cap up on her forehead. "Phil's living, but three other people are dead. And there'll be more. I know there will."

Kate sat flat on the dock deck, unable to move from the wave of weariness which suddenly descended on her. Nora had to be wrong. Her suspicions were overblown and emotional, for good reason. When anything happened to Philip it was a threat to her very existence. They had no children. Their parents were dead. They had been married for twenty-five years and were totally dependent on one another.

But she wasn't a fool, given to bizarre fantasies. The water, churned up by the boat propeller, lapped at the pilings, and somewhere across the marsh an owl hooted. Nora stirred and stood, balancing herself expertly in the swaying boat. She handed up Kate's suitcase and the grocery box and removed Pepper's leash so he could leap from the boat and race to the shore, where he had urgent errands.

"Come spend the night with me," she said. "Your house is probably cold and dark and dusty and mine is warm and I have a roast and a chocolate cake I made for Phil's homecoming. I know you're dead on your feet, so I won't talk to you any more tonight. Things'll keep till morning."

The invitation was tempting. Kate knew her house would be cold and dark and dusty and full of ghosts. She was also dubious about getting the car started.

"Thank you, I will," she said.

The Nobles' house faced the gulf, unlike Kate's, which was a bayside house. The bodies of water nearly met there, and the Nobles kept a rowboat in the little lagoon back of their house for mullet fishing and lazing around the bay, checking on their crab traps. In the front the tall pilings supported a weathered old cypress and cedar structure, and sometimes at high tide the waves of the gulf lapped companionably at the underpinnings. The back wall rested on a sand dune. The house was one of the oldest on the island and had been built in the days before there were setback laws and dune protection regulations. A few steps led up to the back porch, which was screened and held an old round oak table, where the Nobles ate almost every meal in good weather. Nora had boxes filled with petunias and geraniums here, sheltered from the front beach winds and often lasting through the winter. Kate, glancing at them under the porch light, saw that some, if not all, had survived the winter and were in bloom.

The kitchen was warm and fragrant with the smell of roasted meat. A big chocolate cake dominated the wooden counter.

"Put your things in the spare room," Nora said. "I'll find something for Pepper and fix him a bed here in the kitchen."

Kate looked around for the fluffy smoke-colored cat Phil had named Graymalkin, after the witches' cat in Macbeth.

"Where is Graymalkin?" she asked.

"I don't know," Nora said worriedly. "I've been looking for her for a couple of days."

"Tomcats are bad to roam," Kate said, "but she's a lady, isn't she?"

"I hope." Nora grinned. "Phil said *malkin* is Scottish for Matilda."

The Nobles had inherited their furniture and it was more suited to a Victorian town house than to the beach, but it was comfortable and somehow solidly welcoming, Kate thought, looking at the tall oak bed with its crocheted spread. The adjoining bathroom had an old iron-footed tub six feet long and, to Kate's surprise, a rocking chair, a shelf full of books, and an old parlor organ.

She washed her face and hands and swiped at her hair and went out laughing.

"I never saw a parlor organ in a bathroom before," she said. "Nor a rocking chair, nor a bookshelf."

Nora, busy slicing roast beef, smiled.

"I didn't have anyplace else to put them after Phil bought me a real piano. He thought I should take up music again and, of course, the organ's so old and wheezy and out of tune I couldn't play it. So look!"

She pushed open the swinging door into the dining room and living room, and there in the midst of ornately carved love seats and platform rockers was a sleek shining black grand piano.

"Nora! I didn't know you played the piano. This is beautiful!" Kate said, laying a gentle finger on an ivory key.

"I used to, but I gave it up when we moved here. It was Phil's idea that I had made too much of a sacrifice. He fixed up an old plane for Glenn Riley and there was money for this."

"A sweet man," Kate said, and Nora bit her lips and averted her face.

"The best," she said chokily after a moment. "They better let him alone or I'll kill them!"

"Who?" Kate asked gently. "Do you have any idea?"

Nora's face under the gray bangs quivered with uncertainty.

"I don't know. Here, eat. You want mayonnaise or mustard on your sandwich? How about a slice of tomato?"

Kate was suddenly hungry.

Pepper leaned contentedly against her thigh and put a paw on her foot. He knew the Nobles' house as well as Kate's own. Kate turned down the fragrant freshly made coffee, nibbled at a piece of rich chocolate cake, and was glad when Nora said, "Go to bed. We'll talk in the morning."

In her warm nightgown after face washing and tooth brushing, Kate looked in Nora's door.

"Are you sure there are no snakes in here tonight?"

"Don't think I haven't checked," Nora said, restlessly poking at a pillow back of her head. "I'm not morbid about them, but I don't welcome them, either. I suppose I'll be looking to be sure the rest of my life."

"I'm gon' take that up, too," Kate said. "If you got rattlers on the gulf side, I bet they're plentiful on the bay side."

She said it idly, but as Kate walked down the little hall to bed, she knew it must be true. She certainly intended to check.

2

➤F riday morning was warm and sunny, with the sound as placid as a bowl of milk. Nora was in a hurry to go get her husband and had laid out rolls, butter, and marmalade beside Kate's cup and saucer. Tucked under the edge of the pretty flowered plate which held the rolls was a folded piece of paper. On it were three names:

Sarah Langhorne, suicide;
Finley Sawyer, poison;
Paul Lewis (?)

Kate knew all of them slightly except Sarah Langhorne, but she hadn't known that they were dead. She poured a cup of coffee and sat back down and studied the list.

Nora should have told her more ... or less. She had to go and see if her car would start and then open and air her house. It was hard to concentrate on household chores with the piece of paper and those names before her.

She doubted if there was anybody to ask questions of until Nora got home. The island was very quiet in January. The vacant slips at the boat dock the night before told her that. It was possible that some people had flown in. The grassy runway was an invitation to small planes. And some people preferred to beach their boats in front of their houses. Still, she would walk down to the dock and see if she could find a talkative fisherman or at least some mechanical genius who would work his magic on her car, if need be.

A couple of small planes were tied down at the edge of the landing strip. Kate recognized neither of them. A lone fisherman cast from the ferryboat dock and Kate and Pepper walked toward him. Pepper growled deep in his throat and Kate reached for his collar as the fisherman turned.

He glanced casually at Pepper and smiled at Kate.

"Let him go," he said. "I get along with dogs. I'm Greg Herren. Who are you?"

Kate gave her name and started to extend a hand, but she saw that both of his were occupied, one with a rod, the other with a plastic bag of odoriferous shrimp he was using for bait. He glanced helplessly at his hands and laughed. Kate released Pepper, who sniffed at the man, wagged his tail, and trotted toward the beach, where he had a rendezvous with something in the marsh grass.

"You having any luck?" Kate asked the standard question everybody addressed to fishermen.

"Not till now," the man said, laughing. "I've been

told I should meet you. I'm a friend of the Nobles and have heard a lot about the Mulcays."

"New on the island?" Kate asked.

"Six months," he said. "I came down from Wisconsin for a little R&R and I haven't been able to stay away." He cast expertly at the base of one of the big pilings and something immediately pulled his bait under.

"You got a bite!" Kate said unnecessarily.

"Pinfish," he said, reeling in. "Too small to eat, but fine for bait."

A small silver fish wriggled on his hook and he pulled it off and threw it in his bait bucket, wiping his hands on his jeans.

"I'm telling you," he said, "and you must know all about island fishing. You're a property owner, I believe."

Kate nodded. "And I better go see about my property. I haven't been down in more than a year and I don't have any idea what state it's in. Friends and renters. But I don't like to fish," she added.

"You have transportation?" Greg asked.

"I hope so," said Kate. "I haven't tried to start the old buggy yet. But if I know Phil Noble, he has put gas in it and charged up the battery."

The fisherman looked out across the little harbor and cleared his throat. "Phil's been pretty sick," he said. "Bad accident."

"You think it was an accident that snake got in his house?" Kate asked.

He smiled and she noticed for the first time that his eyes, deep in a sun-browned face shadowed by dark eyebrows, were very blue.

"Sure," he said easily. "Nobody would do a thing like that to Phil."

Kate turned toward the parking lot.

"Good luck starting your car," he called after her. "I'd offer a ride or jumper cables—whatever—but I flew down in my Cherokee and I wouldn't be much help."

Kate smiled and shook her head.

The old car did start, promptly, and with a muffler-less roar. Kate blessed Phil. Pepper leaped into the backseat and poked his head close to hers, echoing her surprise and satisfaction with a triumphant whimper.

"Sit down and fasten your seat belt," Kate admonished him.

The old car might have seat belts, but she wouldn't have been able to find them beneath the fishing gear, beer cans, beach towels, and litter left by the previous users. Besides, the speed limit on the island was a satirical twenty miles per hour—as if this car or any of the others she knew well could attain such a high speed.

It was a stylish equipage, all right, Kate thought, looking at the refrigerator paint Benjy had used to deter the rust on the back and sides. It had been white when he applied it, but now it was yellow and Kate suspected the color was rust showing through.

Still, it ran, and she guided it down the winding single-lane road, expertly avoiding the sand beds on either side. It was an island legend that anybody who budged on Ila got stuck in the sand and it had happened to her many times, particularly after an autumn hurricane had passed that way, rearranging the terrain. Now she drove at a noisy but sedate pace, the windows down, originally to enable her to breathe deeply of the gulf breezes and the pungent smell of beach cedar and pine and rosemary which lined the road, silver-gray clumps touched by lavender blooms, even now, in winter. But today she needed air because the hole in the back floorboard let up noxious fumes from the exhaust and she didn't want to take time to arrange a tin sign that a storm had washed up and she had put over the hole. It was a fine make-do patch, but it shifted from time to time and had to be repositioned. But with the windows down she only got a whiff of the hot exhaust breath herself, and Pepper already had his head out the window.

The two-mile trip subtly cheered Kate. The long-legged houses on stilts along the gulf beach seemed to be deserted and she met no cars on the road. Cars meeting always had to stop and reconnoiter, one of them picking the closest driveway to back into and let the other by. It made for pleasant socializing. In fact, Eulalie Desmond always invited everybody she met on the road to lunch. Sometimes it was a strain when she met six people and all of them accepted and she only had two mullet for lunch. Her husband, Geordie, had to hastily check his crab traps and make a run on the nearest neighbors' freezers. Doors were always left unlocked on Ila, and it was generally accepted that borrowers would take what they needed, meticulously—mostly— returning the take next passing.

Today Kate was glad she met no one. She didn't want to be slowed down. She needed to look over the cottage, put up her groceries, change to blue jeans, and get back to the dock in time to meet Nora and Phil. It might be that in Phil's weakened state Nora would need help getting him to the house. Of course there was the new man, Greg Herren, but he might have put up his fishing gear and gone home. Kate thought about him. He really was extremely handsome, she decided, those blue eyes and black brows and probably dark hair under his floppy fishing hat. He was tall and broad-shouldered; he wore his checked shirt tucked in, his slacks belted, evidence that he was lean. She guessed his age at mid- to late forties and decided that he had a nice smile, although he hadn't really bestirred himself to help her get her car going, as almost any islander would have. If they couldn't actually do anything, they came and stood around, offering suggestions and speculations and a kind of comfort if the difficulty warranted it.

Kate decided she really loved the island and most islanders no matter what pain of remembering, what loneliness for Benjy might attack her. The murmur of the gulf surf, often stormy and tumultuous, assured her it was going to be a calm day, and she could use calm.

Following the road that forked off to the bayside, she started counting driveways, an old habit from foggy weather when that guided them home: Dr. Wells, a professor of some kind of biology at the university; Mary Darden, a social worker in Apalachicola; Deb and Dab (for Debbie and Dabney) Winkler, two cute rich kids who apparently did nothing but play in the water, swimming, sunning, sailing a catamaran in the sound waters in the summertime and a thirty-foot cruiser to the Bahamas during the winter months; then there were

Jim Preston, a retired forest ranger, and his wife, Emmy, who was an amateur but terribly enthusiastic marine biologist and had the best collection of seashells on the gulf coast.

"Five," murmured Kate, and turned in the shell driveway to her own cottage. Pulverized by the wheels of cars and summer suns and winter freezes, three loads of oyster shells hauled from the cannery on the shore had worked their way into the sand, making a fairly firm and steady driveway. From time to time you had to rake back the scattered oyster shells and Kate hadn't done that in a long time. If she had time ... For the first time she thought she might like to stay on Ila for an extended visit. She loved oyster shell driveways, the way they matched the sand in whiteness, iridescent on a moonlit night.

She sat a moment in the driveway after she had turned off the smelly roar of the car and looked at her and Benjy's house. It was small, not as small as she had originally planned. She had told the man who sold them the lot that all she really wanted was a screened porch and a fireplace.

"Okay," he said. "You can camp out if you want to. The only building requirement on the island is that you put your house on pilings and have at least a thousand feet under roof. You want a screened porch that big?"

"Well, with a kitchen and a bathroom," Kate had said dreamily.

Benjy had held out for a bedroom, then two bedrooms and a biggish living room–kitchen to accommodate the fireplace, but he had acquiesced to her desire for a big screened porch. They had two, one across the front with a little walkway crossing the dunes and linking it to the beach fifty feet away, and a back one with space for a wooden shower stall for swimmers, and racks for fishing gear. It was the perfect house, they decided, hanging a hammock at the corner of the porch where it would catch the best breeze and have a view of passing barges and sailboats and the lights in Simolona at night. It was even a pretty house, they decided, coming back to it from a sunset walk and catching a view of it tucked back of the dunes, its rough cedar walls bathed in coral light.

Looking at it now, Kate decided the pine tree which shaded the back porch had grown since she had seen it last, and those that framed the view of the bay from the front porch were now visible over the rooftop. Only the old wind-stunted live oaks with their twisted gray trunks remained the same, beautiful as bonsai.

"Well, come on, lazy," she said to Pepper. "Let's get in and get busy."

She picked up the box of groceries and climbed the steps to the back door. Pepper raced madly around the house to investigate the beach and deal sharply with pelicans and herons that might be trespassing there. There was a table by the back door and Kate deposited her groceries there while she wrestled with the kitchen door—not locked, of course, but swollen by rains and stuck. She pulled it hard and as it came open, she heard a door on the front of the house rattle.

For a moment she stood there, oddly uneasy. Then

she remembered the doors had that trick. When the back door was opened or closed, the front door rattled in response.

"Hello, house," she called out as she entered the kitchen. Suddenly something black flashed across the bedroom at eye level. Airborne and big, she thought incredulously.

She walked timidly toward the bedroom door and a hideous nauseating stench engulfed her.

The bed, the floor, the dresser were filled with stinking little piles of cat excrement!

Kate was backing out when she saw through the closet door two green eyes glittering in the darkness at hat shelf level.

"Come out of there, cat!" she called sternly. "You get out of this house!"

She looked around for the broom—anything to poke at it. Fortunately, somebody had left a dust mop leaning against the kitchen cabinet nearest her. She took a grip on it and walked carefully—to avoid the nasty piles— toward the closet door.

"Kitty, kitty!" she called persuasively. "Come out, kitty."

Nervously she edged closer, reaching inside the closet door for the light switch. A huge black cat sat in the middle of the highest shelf, hissing at her, showing fearsome teeth, and growling deep in its throat.

"Kitty, kitty," Kate said weakly.

This was no kitty. It was a wild cat, one of the feral felines that had multiplied on the island recently, roaming dunes and woods like sinister brigands. She meant to back away, but she dropped the mop and the noise electrified the cat. Feeling cornered in the closet, it let out a snarl and lunged for Kate's head.

The claws raked her head and dug into her face. Instinctively fearing for her eyes, Kate screamed and pulled at the black fur with all her strength.

Pepper, dripping from an impromptu swim, responded.

He catapulted himself into the house and nearly knocked Kate down when he caught sight of the cat in her face. His snarl diverted the cat and it gave up on Kate and dropped like a sack of knives to Pepper's back.

Yelping, Pepper raced for the backyard. Unable to shake the cat off or to get it within biting range, Pepper did the next best thing. He headed for the beach and dashed into the water.

Only then did the cat let go. Pepper grabbed it by the throat, shaking it fiercely and dunking it in the incoming waves.

Kate, busy trying to stanch the blood from her face and hand wounds, did not look to see what happened to the cat.

An hour later Nora Noble drove into the yard.

"You've got to have a rabies shot," she said firmly. "Come on, I'm taking you to Simolona."

"This mess!" wailed Kate. "How will I ever be able to stand my house again?"

"Never mind," said Nora. "We'll clean it up when we get back."

"What about Phil?"

"Aw, Phil." Nora smiled. "He feels so good he wanted to get a haircut and visit our lawyer. Lem Parrish is over there and offered to bring him home later this afternoon."

They had crossed the sound, tied up the boat, and were in Nora's car headed for the nearest roadside emergency clinic before the attack of the wild cat was mentioned.

"How do you think he got in my house?" Kate asked.

"I think it was *put* in your house," Nora said.

"But why?" asked Kate. "From the looks of the mess it must have been shut in there a long time."

"It's something to look into," Nora offered. "Maybe it'll give you some idea when it happened. As for why, I don't know. That's something I hope you will find out. Why was that snake put in Phil's room? Why did sweet, trusting little Sarah Langhorne wade out into the cut where they're catching sharks and never show up again? Why was Finley Sawyer's drinking water poisoned? And Paul Lewis ... Kate, he was found dead in his boat in a boathouse over at Simolona, lying in the bottom with his hands crossed on his chest. No sign of injury. Cause of death, you know the old thing, heart failure."

It didn't make Kate's lacerations feel any better to consider this string of deaths. She didn't think she was a candidate for murder. A wild house cat was not a dependable killer. But by the time she'd had stitches in her scalp, one on her wrist, and one athwart her left cheek, she wasn't sure.

True to her promise, Nora returned to the stomach-turning fray and helped Kate clean up. They stripped the bed and spread the bedding on the deck and turned the hose on it. When the fecal matter was washed away, they tackled the sheets and quilts with brooms and soap powder.

Kate grieved that the prettiest quilt of all, one Benjy had bought in the mountains for her Christmas present, had served as the coverlet and was the cat's chief target. But the soap powder and hose did not seem to dim the bright red, white, and blue seven-pointed star in the center or the smaller stars that made the quilt's border. It came out looking blithe and bouyant in the sunshine and when it had dripped sufficiently to make it easy to move, they hauled it to the washing machine and started over. The floor was easier, soap suds and scrubbing brushes and elbow grease, and by midafternoon cleanliness and the wholesome smell of good scrubbing had replaced the cat stench.

"I'm just glad he confined himself to one room," Kate said tiredly.

"He could do that," Nora pointed out, "because a bag of dog food was nearby in the kitchen for him to eat and your bathroom was here so he could drink water out of the toilet."

They had seen paw prints on the white porcelain bowl and they felt a momentary twinge of sympathy for a wild animal trapped. But how did he get in? Who opened the door and who closed it?

"I didn't know feral cats had become such a problem on Ila," Kate said.

"Awful," Nora said. "You remember when the island

had but one stray cat? A black and white fellow with a smear on his upper lip that looked like Hitler's mustache? Everybody fed him and called him Hitler and then he turned out to be Eva and had a litter of kittens. Somebody adopted the whole kit and kaboodle and took them home with them. But there must have been others that were left behind or abandoned. Now there are dozens of them and they travel in packs. They've been terrible on the birds."

Nora invited Kate back to her house for supper, but the slashes on her face and scalp, deeper than those on her arms, were paining her and Kate decided to take a pill the doctor had given her and crawl into the guest room bed. The cat hadn't defiled that room and it was not as full of memories as the room that had been hers and Benjy's.

After all the months since his death she still had not learned to sleep in the middle of the bed. She stuck to what had been her side and was still surprised to put out a hand at night and find the other side smooth and empty.

3

►The doctor's pain pill had given her deep and dreamless sleep. She did not awaken until Pepper, who slept on an old beach towel by the kitchen door, stuck his muzzle in her face and whined to get out.

The sun was rising out of the Gulf of Mexico across the island, a great fiery globe that spilled a pathway of liquid gold across the blue water and stained the sky with rose. Ila Island sunrises, Kate thought contentedly as she rinsed out the percolator and started her coffee, were spectacular, second only to sunsets, which were an end-of-the-day marvel on the bay side of the island. She took personal pride in the fact that because more trees grew on the bay side and the dunes, which were not regularly lashed and sometimes leveled by storms, like those on the gulf side, sunsets were framed in black lace. It was one of the reasons she and Benjy had chosen to build on the bay instead of on the gulf, which was considered more choice and more expensive real estate. They made a point of getting to the front porch for their first drink of the day in time to watch the sun sink beyond the tall pines at Heron Point.

The kitchen–living room they had built pleased her. Pecky cypress covered the walls, and a curved and satin-smooth length of driftwood they had picked up and hauled home from the western beach hung over the work island with pegs to hold pots. The last visitors, friends of Tallahassee friends, had left the kitchen neat, and after she had made and eaten a piece of toast and drunk two cups of coffee, Kate walked outside for a look at the yard.

All the windows needed washing. They always did, because of the salt spray, but she felt compelled to visit the Nobles pretty soon, allowing time for their late-abedness and leisurely breakfast. She wouldn't start any housecleaning projects.

She had tried to have shrubs and flowers on the island, but except for those nature bestowed on the sand, nothing grew. Swamp myrtle with its fragrant bronze leaves and blue-black berries was a favorite of hers, and they had transplanted six fine bushy shrubs from a nursery in the little inland town of Sopchoppy. A month later a hurricane swept the island, sending water from the gulf to the very steps of her cottage, and the swamp myrtle drowned. Daylilies thrived once in the old oak half whiskey barrel by the steps, but with nobody there to water them, they had shriveled and died. The barrel staves dried out and fell apart like an unfolding flower.

The little utility room beneath the house had a

washer and a dryer, a second refrigerator for overflow drinks and ice, and a few garden tools.

Nature had been generous with rosemary and beach cedar, the dark green and shapely shrubs which reminded her of the boxwood in a Virginia cavalier garden. Clumps of pearl gray goldenrod still held the drying bloom heads, remnants of November's beach goldenrod blooming season, which was a breathtaking sight for a whole month every fall. The little shrubs, unlike any goldenrod Kate had ever seen, drew clouds of Monarch butterflies on their way to their winter spawning grounds in Mexico. Clumps of palmettos were an enhancement to the center of the island—also the home of rattlesnakes, Nora said, but Kate often cut a palmetto frond or two for a green arrangement in the cottage and had never seen a snake. Red-berried yaupon with its gray branches and elegant little dark green leaves was a year-round temptation to her. Once she had planned a yaupon hedge between the cottage and the road, but Benjy's cancer had weakened him beyond the point of digging up the shrubs and excavating planting holes. She had given up and collected red-berried branches on walks, arranging them in a basket for a centerpiece on the kitchen table.

Now she was pleased to notice that the yaupon bush which was there when they bought the lot had a scattering of ruby-bright berries. Maybe, come the spring ...

Beneath the house Kate stopped by the dryer to take out her quilt. For a wonder it was immaculate, even clean-smelling. She was folding it when she noticed that the window on the east side of the utility room was open and its screen was missing. She thought she would certainly have noticed that the day before when she brought the quilt down. But then, under the stress of the cat's attack she might not have looked.

She went outside and looked now. The screen was on the ground and, oddly enough, the sand beneath the window showed no tracks but had been raked smooth with the lawn rake which leaned against the wall. The rake marks went all the way out to where pine needles carpeted the ground and made tracks impossible.

Kate was puzzled.

Surely she would have heard, or Pepper would have heard and sounded an alarm, if anybody had removed the screen and opened the window the night before. And why would anybody want entrance to that little utility room? There was nothing in it to interest a thief. In fact, the door remained unlocked year-round, an invitation to anybody who needed a certain size screwdriver or a handful of nails to help themselves.

The wind could have blown the screen out, but how did the window get raised? How did the sand get such a careful raking?

Kate picked up the quilt and pulled the door shut. Its rusty hinges creaked protestingly and that may have been why the window was chosen for entrance. She hurried up the steps with the idea of calling the Nobles with the radio on her refrigerator, but the radio was already blaring her name.

* * *

"Kate! Kate!" cried Nora's voice. "Come quick, come quick! Oh, please hurry." She broke into a sob. "Phil's dead!"

Kate hurried into jeans and sweatshirt and without washing her face or brushing her teeth or combing her hair she hit the road. She spotted a group of men standing at the edge of the landing strip and realized that was where Phil must be. She pulled onto the grass and ran toward them.

Nora was on her knees beside him, and the new man, Greg Herren, had just finished trying to give him mouth-to-mouth resuscitation. Kate could tell it was useless, and she knelt down beside Nora and put her arms around her.

Nora buried her face in Kate's shoulder, weeping convulsively. Kate looked up at Greg.

"What happened?"

He moved his shoulders in weary negation. "I don't know. I don't know. Another heart attack?"

It was a question and Nora answered it vehemently. "No! Somebody ... killed ... him!"

"Oh, honey," Kate said, patting her shoulder and digging out a crumpled Kleenex for her streaming eyes. "Let's wait and see."

As if on cue, *Mercy Bird*, a helicopter that clucked and sidled in awkwardly like a crippled rooster, came out of the northern sky and landed fifty feet away.

"I radioed them," Greg said, "as soon as I saw."

Two medics leaped out of the craft before its blades were still and, crouching, ran toward the group around

Phil's body. One of them carried a stretcher, the other an oxygen tank.

But it was futile, Kate knew. They eased Phil's body onto the stretcher and one of them turned to Nora. "You'll want to come with us?"

"Yes!" Nora cried. "Kate ...?"

But before Kate could volunteer, Greg Herren said, "I'd better come with you, Nora. I have a car at the airport in Tallahassee. We can come back in that. Maybe there are things at your house Kate could see to."

Nora gulped. "Turn off the pots ... whatever ... in the kitchen. I was cooking breakfast when I heard Phil scream."

Kate nodded. "Do you want me to take the boat to Simolona and call anybody? I can meet you there when you come home."

Nora shook her head. "I can't think. I don't know. Maybe the sheriff's office in Apalachicola."

The helicopter bearing her friend's body was airborne before Kate began to cry. Hurrying toward the Nobles' house and what she feared might be a smoldering kitchen fire from a burning pot, she continued crying. Phil Noble was a good man, a gentle man. He had come to Atlanta during Benjy's final illness and stood by in case he was needed. When she was too exhausted to stay awake by Benjy's bedside in the hospital, she dozed off with her head resting on her arms at the foot of the bed. When she awakened, it was to find Philip Noble sitting on the other side of the bed, his hand on Benjy's thin, wasted hand.

Phil had been the only civilian pallbearer she had

wanted for Benjy. The others were old friends from the police department, where he had served for thirty years.

Now Phil was gone, too, and it seemed almost more than she could bear. But she didn't have time to think about it. A black cloud of smoke and the smell of burning grease reached out to her from the Nobles' kitchen. The bacon in an iron skillet had caught fire. The reek of scorched metal and charred food choked her. Kate turned off the stove and grabbed a potholder and hauled the ruined utensils to the backyard. She opened the windows and the kitchen door and turned on the ceiling fan to sweep out the smoke and smell.

She walked through the house and saw that Nora had already made up their bed, and their nightclothes hung on a hook on the closet door. On the back porch the table was set with a pretty cloth and silver and dishes for two. A Christmas cactus, full of crimson satin blooms, was in the middle of the table in an old soup tureen, Nora's welcome-home-to-Philip touch.

Kate choked and began picking up the dishes. Nora wouldn't need a reminder that there would not be breakfast for two now. Running them under the hot water tap to get rid of the residue of smoke, Kate dried them and put them away.

The men who had clustered around Philip's body on the landing strip had dispersed, moving off toward the dock and their boats or walking down the beach toward their cottages. One, an old islander named Ash Olsen, came toward the Nobles' house to meet Kate.

Ash had been a turpentiner on Ila Island long before Old Lady Sanderson, who owned the canneries and several of the shrimp boats and most of the real estate in Simolona, had bought it for peanuts during the Depression with the idea of turning it into a winter resort. She wanted to call it Little Riviera and had built a landing strip for the planes of wealthy lookers and brought in an architect, who drew pretty pictures of streets and a golf course and a swimming pool and a clubhouse.

None of it had taken. Only old turpentiners like Ash, who lived in a shack at the western end of the island in a forest of scarred-faced pine trees, had remained. And the people who came did not care anything about the Riviera or a clubhouse or a golf course. They simply wanted cheap land for simple cottages and good fishing. By that time Old Lady Sanderson had lost interest in developing a Cracker Cannes and gone off to Europe with a handsome young hairdresser, who had picked up a French accent in Boys Town. She died there and the hairdresser had taken up with a ski instructor, and the island was sold for taxes to three Tallahassee college professors. One of them was allergic to sun and hated fishing and subsequently sold his share to the Nobles.

The turpentiners' contract with Mrs. Sanderson had long since expired, and they had loaded their barrels of resin on barges, hauled them to a still in Simolona, and moved up in Georgia, where there were bigger and better long-leafed yellow pines.

Only Ash remained. He was a little man, grizzled and sun-cured, and he lived alone in a two-room shack sheltered by pines and tucked under what the islanders satirically called The Mountain, a section of gulf beach where the dunes had survived winds and tides for a hundred or more years and attained a height of twenty-five or thirty feet. They were certainly mountainous by comparison with the terrain which was sea level or less. They were held in place by young pines, beach cedar, and palmetto. The dunes made a pearly white wall between Ash and the chilly north wind and served to hide him from game wardens, who did not understand why the big sea turtles which came in from the gulf laid so few eggs, and were vigilant about enforcing seasons for catching bluefish and mackerel.

Narcotics agents had considered Ash's place a good prospect as drop point for drugs, but after one or two visits with him during which he read them Scripture and had them singing "Amazing Grace" in a room pungent with the smell of smoking mullet and unwashed overalls, they put him down as a nut and forgot about him.

Ash lived by fishing and trapping coons and rattlesnakes. If he had need of a few eggs when the big turtles' nests were handy, he borrowed them, as he believed the Fisherman of Galilee intended. He was never greedy. Turtle eggs were a little fishy-tasting and a dozen or so a season sufficed. Riding the channel in his leaky old skiff, he netted shrimp and tonged for oysters when the summer people ordered them, always keeping a good supply for himself. And in spring and summer he varied his diet with beach greens and the delicate young shoots of smilax and blackberries which abounded at the edge of the landing strip.

For cash, which he did not seem to regard highly, an occasional storm deposited salable objects on his beach—lawn furniture which had washed in from yards on the shore or neighboring islands, oars, gasoline cans from boats, a fine slender mast from a sailboat, once a snowy canvas sail which made a durable roof between his house and his privy. He liked to sit in its shade to shell shrimp or shuck oysters. Once the beneficent tides had endowed Ash with a leaky, storm-splintered canoe. No longer seaworthy, it lay upturned beside Ash's shack for months before Kate saw it and coveted it for a planter in her backyard.

Ash sold it to her for $3 and Benjy, laughing at the whim of both buyer and seller, towed it home for her and helped her fill it with rich soil which mushroom growers on the shore sold to gardeners after a crop or two of the succulent mushrooms. Geraniums liked the heat and made do with whatever moisture the summer rains brought. But in the press of Benjy's illness and her absence from the island, they had shriveled and died.

Kate thought of them now as she saw Ash approaching with an old brown croaker sack in his hands. She looked closely and saw the sack writhe with a life of its own.

"Ash!" she called out peremptorily. "Have you got a snake in that sack?"

"Hidy-do, Kate," the old man said, ignoring her question. "I come to see what I could do for Nora and—" he gulped, "Philip. I plumb reverenced that man. I want to hep any way I can."

Good reason, Kate thought with a touch of cynicism. Phil was the one who made it possible for Ash to stay on the island. The other owners rightly called him a squatter and wanted to clear the island of his trashy abode. Phil named him nightwatchman and caretaker, two meaningless titles, but because of Phil's support, the others permitted him to remain.

"I don't know what anybody can do," Kate said sadly, looking out at the little harbor where the Nobles' pristine white boat bobbed and turned in the incoming tide with the grace of a pinafored young girl dancing. "I guess we'll wait to hear from Nora about a funeral and all. I've got to call the sheriff in Apalachicola and ... I don't know."

Her eyes returned to Ash's croaker sack.

"Ash, you got a snake in there?"

The old man aimed a stream of tobacco juice at a goldenrod. "Two of 'em," he said. "Mocs."

"Moccasins? Cottonmouths?" persisted Kate.

"Yep, two beauties. Want to see?"

"No! No!" cried Kate. "Take 'em away."

"I mean to," said Ash with dignity. He turned away and then turned back. "You tell Nora I'm here if she can use me—for ary thing. If Phil is gon' be buried on the island, I'll be proud to dig the grave."

Kate nodded. She knew the words did not mean pleasure but honor. He would be honored to dig his friend's grave.

Ash had gone but a little distance down the path to the beach when Kate called him back.

"Ash, did Phil see those snakes?"

The old man turned to face her squarely. "No, ma'am!" he said emphatically. "You reckon I'd do that to

Phil? Why, he's the biggest reason I hunt snakes. If I could rid the island of 'em, it would be all the better for him."

Kate nodded again. "But cottonmouths, Ash. What do you do with them? Why don't you just kill them?"

"People buys them," Ash said. "They don't keer if they no damn good—and they ain't. Now, you take a rattler—"

"*You* take a rattler," said Kate, smiling for the first time. "I've got to go call the sheriff and see if I can reach Nora at the hospital."

Even if she didn't have such sad errands to do, she didn't want a lesson in herpetology from Ash. She knew as well as Ash did that he skinned and tanned the hides of the rattlesnakes and sold them to some middleman up in Georgia after milking them of their venom. She had heard that he also ran a small business in alligator hides, although they were protected. Benjy had worried that the old man was violating the wild game law, but when an eight-foot gator ate an islander's dog and nearly got a small child, Benjy turned his back on Ash's enterprise. He was affirmed in that decision when a game warden told him, with some satisfaction, that there must be five hundred little gators growing in the island's swamp area.

The sheriff, reached by marine radio, said he had called Tallahassee and learned the official cause of Phil's death was a heart attack. He expressed sympathy to the widow and friends and no further interest. Kate was able to reach Nora at the hospital and found her so limp and debilitated she could hardly talk. Greg Herren came on the phone and it was apparent he had taken charge.

"I'll bring Nora back to the island tomorrow," he said. "After she has completed arrangements for getting Phil's body home. She wants the funeral to be there. She's going to spend the night at the home of some friends—Harrell, Harris?" He fumbled for the name.

"Harris," said Kate. "I know them. I can call her there if there's anything to settle here. Suppose I plan to bring her boat over to Simolona to meet you all around noon tomorrow?"

"Super," Greg said, and Kate, punching the off switch on the radio, made a face. She hated people who said "super" when they meant yes or all right or sure or fine or even okay.

Kate decided to go early to Simolona. There would be things to do there for Nora. The first thing she thought of from her newspaperwoman's experience was to notify the little weekly paper, which would go to press on Tuesday. There would be friends of the Nobles in the grocery and hardware stores and, of course, the ferry-boat captain. She remembered that Nora had said Phil stopped off on their way back from the hospital to see his lawyer and she wondered which of two who had offices over the drugstore might be the one. The court-house was twenty miles away, but the two lawyers had homes overlooking the sound from Simolona's shore and they maintained offices there. She would see, noti-fying them both if she found them.

She went back to her house to change her clothes and get her purse and set out a bowl of water for Pepper on the screened porch. She surveyed her kitchen shelves, thinking ahead to food for those who would come to the funeral. An after-obsequies spread was customary even on the island, where supplies were often short. Once, she remembered, the sons of Elias Banks, an old citizen of the island, had hurried out to cast for mullet, even as his body awaited burial, in order to have a fish fry for their friends afterward. She would get something and, of course, those who came would bring their cakes and covered dishes.

Phil's old fishing hat on the dash of the Nobles' boat gave her a twinge as she stood on the dock preparing to go across. The motor sputtered and was reluctant to start and two fishermen over by the ferry dock came to attention in the time-honored way of islanders.

If a lady-person, as Ash called her, couldn't start a boat, there were men-persons who were alert to her problem and would likely come to her aid. Kate waved back the two fishermen, who prepared to put down their rods, and studied the dash of the boat. It was newer and different from her and Benjy's old boat, and it had been years since she had driven that one.

She pulled the choke. *Let not my right hand forget its cunning,* she prayed silently, and wondered who she was quoting. Psalms, probably, something to do with forgetting Jerusalem. And that reminded her that they would need a minister. Did Nora have one in mind? She should get back to the tiny weathered chapel on the island and sweep out sand and find some greenery in the January absence of flowers. Nora, she knew from long acquaintance, would prefer palmetto fronds and swamp myrtle and smilax to beribboned "floral offerings" from a store on the mainland. Kate would take the liberty of putting "no flowers" in the funeral notice.

The town of Simolona, hot for midwinter, was sleeping in the early afternoon sunshine. In summer the heat was heavy and oppressive, despite its nearness to the gulf. Perversely, Kate felt, it was dank and cold in the wintertime—but not today. Bert, the redheaded kid who helped out at the marina, heard her approach in the river and was on the dock, prepared to grasp the line she threw him and ease the little boat into a mooring.

"Heard about Mr. Noble," he said by way of greeting. "Tough. He is—was—a fine fellow."

Kate stood up and nodded. "How did you hear?" she asked.

"On the radio," he said. "They interrupted the rock program on that Tallahassee station to announce it. They were talking about it at the drugstore, too. Seems like he was pretty important."

"Ah, yes," Kate said, sighing. "He was important, all right."

4

➤ The one business street in town, unlike some of the coast's fishing villages, was pretty. Kindled by the energy and enthusiasm of Nora and Phil, garden club members had planted palms along the sidewalk and wangled park benches from the city government for a green area overlooking the harbor. In spring the mimosa trees would lift a canopy of silky rose and gold blooms and the wild clematis, now frosted with silver seed heads, would cover the little bandstand.

Nora and Phil had pitched in for the backbreaking job of hauling off old crab traps and fish boxes and planting grass and flowers along the banks of the river. Where they had hauled away chunks of broken concrete, remnants of a fish house long since swept away by a hurricane, wildflowers came back, the pink and orange lantana and the heart-lifting trefoil blue blossoms of the St. John's wort, wild daisies, Queen Anne's lace, and the fragile pink windflowers.

The flowers weren't in evidence in January, but the

grass was green and neat, and small flights of concrete steps, which led at intervals to the moorings of small boats, were washed clean by the tannin-brown river water. The fishing smacks and shrimp boats were tied up at the street's end where the deeper water curved, but pleasure craft and small boats like the Nobles' were tethered along the little parkway, which reached to the marina.

Kate stood a moment savoring the day and the proud little town, which Phil had loved second only to the island and would now see no more.

The redheaded boy stood beside her, waiting to see if she had any bundles he could help her with.

"Nothing yet," Kate said, smiling at his eagerness to be helpful. "But I'll have to go to the grocery store before I go back to the island and I'll have a load then, if you're around."

"Yes'm," he said. "I'll be around. I thought I might fish some."

At that moment a red pickup truck with two boys his age pulled up and stopped.

"Hey, Bert," called one of them, "hear about old man Noble? Dead!"

Then, seeing the boat back of Kate, he gulped and turned red.

"That's his boat, ain't it?" he asked uneasily.

Bert nodded. "And this lady is their good friend."

"Okay!" said the boy, and muttered something to his companion at the wheel, who pushed the truck into drive and scratched off.

"Who are they?" asked Kate.

"Aw, them Pinsons. They hate everybody who tries to do something to make Simolona nice. Their daddy wanted to put a freezer plant here and he's been mad ever since Mr. Noble persuaded the county board to make it a park. Had to go across the river to the marsh and it's gon' cost him more."

Kate felt a quickening of interest. Maybe Phil had an enemy in Mr. Pinson.

"Pretty mad at Mr. Noble, I guess," she offered casually.

"Aw, you know how it is," Bert said, examining the float on his line. "Everybody in Simolona thinks the people on the island are stuck-up."

"Stuck-up!" Kate had to laugh. It was such an old-fashioned word for snobbery. She hadn't heard it in years. She had never really known any snobs.

"Why would they think that?"

"Aw, you know," Bert said uncomfortably. "I reckon you all got more money. A house over there and a house somewhere else and better boats."

"Well, the Nobles don't have a house anywhere else. They chose the island as their home and they work very hard to keep a house there, and this boat ..." She glanced at it over her shoulder. "It certainly isn't any yacht."

"That's what my mother says," Bert said. "But you know ... people don't like people interfering."

Kate nodded gravely. She remembered that Bert's mother was a schoolteacher and therefore probably educated above local insecurities and suspicions of snobbery.

"Thank you for helping me, Bert," she said, moving away. "Give my best to your mother. I'll probably see you later. Catch some fish, now."

The boy grinned and bobbed his head and Kate walked toward the drugstore, the social center of the little town, where everybody met twice a day for coffee and gossip. It was one of the few old-time drugstores that Kate knew about, replete with a marble soda fountain, where the ice cream and sodas tasted real instead of like the chalky concoctions she encountered in other places.

The round tables with the wire-backed chairs were vacant at the moment. She was too early or too late for the coffee gatherings.

"Hello, Dr. Joe!" she called to the gray-haired man who sat in a swivel chair back of the prescription counter, reading the *Tallahassee Democrat*. He tilted to his feet and came to meet her.

"Miss Kate!" he said with old-fashioned courtesy which decreed that any woman over sixteen years of age be called "Miss." "I'm so glad you are here. Miss Nora is going to need you. You heard, of course?"

Kate nodded. "I was over there. I don't understand why it happened, Doc. He was just out of the hospital and appeared to be doing well. Nora said he felt so good he stopped in Simolona for a prowl around yesterday when she brought him home from the hospital. Did you see him? Did he seem okay?"

"I did and he was as usual. In good spirits and strong. He had a cup of coffee with me and then he went upstairs to see Cecil James, who lawyers for him. I heard him climbing the stairs and he certainly didn't walk like a sick man. Pug Lindsey was in here this morning and he said he gave him a haircut yesterday and Phil was talking up a fishing trip."

He sighed and turned philosophical: "You never know the day or the hour. I'm a lot older than Phil and I'm beginning to wonder when I'll get my exit visa."

"Oh, don't talk like that, Doc," Kate said, making the obligatory protest. "Simolona and Ila Island can't do without you.

"You give an old man more credit than he deserves, Miss Kate. How about a chocolate ice-cream soda?"

It was too much, too rich. She didn't need it. But Doc's chocolate ice-cream sodas were fizzy and tasted of real chocolate and real cream, and Kate realized that she hadn't eaten since the night before in Nora's kitchen.

"You're on, Doc," she said, taking a stool and resting her arms on the cool marble counter. "I guess I ought to go see the Nobles' lawyer. Maybe Nora's called about funeral plans. I'll need my strength for climbing the stairs."

The old gentleman in his immaculate white coat, matching the carefully slicked-down white hair, reached for a glass dish and his ice-cream scoop and said thoughtfully, "Be a big turnout from Tallahassee, I imagine. You all might want to charter the ferry to take the crowd over. I'll close the store out of respect, of course."

"That's nice of you," Kate said.

"Philip was a friend. Not much business anyhow," he added candidly. "Movement to make me close up the soda fountain or get a restaurant license. Phil went to bat for me, but you can't buck that Tallahassee crowd. And drugs ... nearly everybody goes to that new Wal-Mart up the road for discount goods now. I mainly stay open to take care of old folks and babies. Get sick in the night and can't go that far."

"Oh, Doc," Kate said in a rush of sympathy. He and his drugstore were Simolona fixtures, beloved by everybody. The little store with old curved-glass-fronted cabinets and its fragrance of wintergreen and freshly made coffee had been there a hundred years, since lumber barons floated the big pine and cypress logs down the river to the little railroad that once hugged the coastline. Phil and Nora had loved its ornate facade with the weathered apothecary sign swinging over the door and had persuaded Doc not to change it when the garden club set Simolona on a general paint-up and repair kick that misguidedly went in for modernization.

The soda was as good as Kate knew it would be, and she felt subtly cheered for having nourishment. She stood up to go and opened her purse.

"No, you don't, young lady," Doc said. "This one is on the house. And the next one will be, too, if death-watch don't get me."

Kate looked at him in puzzlement.

"Deathwatch?" she said.

"Oh, you know the old story," the old pharmacist said, laughing but without humor. "There's a little brown beetle that eats drugs. Call 'em deathwatches. They say when you hear them knocking their heads against the wood at night, death is coming to your house."

"Don't tell me you've heard them," scoffed Kate.

"Every day," said Doc Joe. "Every day, every evening, right back there where the controlled substances are stored."

"They're probably all drugged up," Kate said, laughing. "And they don't know what they're foretelling, if anything."

"I know," Doc said. "I know."

Kate climbed outside stairs to the offices of Cecil James, the lawyer. He had no secretary on duty in the small front office. She had not met him before and she was surprised to find a young man in his twenties or early thirties intent on a computer in the larger back office. The back office, facing the street and the harbor, had a small balcony big enough for a couple of plastic chairs and a long-legged telescope. The French doors were closed against the freshening breeze from the sound, but Kate could imagine that in a couple of months there might be flowers on the balcony and a wonderful view of blue water and live oak trees.

"Mr. James," she said from the doorway as the young lawyer looked up. "I'm Kate Mulcay, a friend of the Nobles."

"Oh, yes!" he cried, jumping up. "I know you. I went to Emory law school and I read the Atlanta papers. Nora Noble sent word that you might be dropping by."

As he talked, he hurried to offer his hand and push a chair toward Kate. Since he had mentioned Atlanta newspapers, Kate thought belatedly that she should call in and tell the city editor, Shell Shelnutt, that she might be detained. Phil's death probably wouldn't be news in

Atlanta, but she would offer it to the obit desk anyhow and she assumed the undertaker in Tallahassee would put a notice in the *Democrat.*

"Have you talked to Nora since Phil died?" Kate asked.

"Not to Nora, to Greg Herren. He called for her. She wants the funeral day after tomorrow and she asked that you and I handle things at this end. I have a launch big enough to take the coffin across and I can talk to the cap'n about chartering the ferry for friends, if you think well of it."

Doc Joe had mentioned the ferryboat, too, Kate reflected. It must be the pattern for island funerals.

"There's also the matter of pallbearers and a minister," the young lawyer said.

"Yes," said Kate, her eyes on the little balcony with its telescope. "You seem to have thought of everything."

The young man coughed apologetically and Kate turned her attention back to him. He wore a dark suit and a white shirt, formal wear for downtown Simolona, even in the wintertime, and his hair was longish but carefully combed back into a flounce over his collar. His glasses, undoubtedly chosen to give him the appearance of age, were rimless and delicately tinted. He seemed very young to handle the role of family counselor to the Nobles. He would probably mention the reading of the will next, she thought.

"About the arrangements," he said hesitantly. "My family is in the funeral business up in Georgia and I guess you'd say I'm experienced."

"Good," said Kate. "I'll leave it up to you. I'll just

pick up Nora here tomorrow. And the funeral meats ... I guess I should think of that."

"It's customary," he said.

Kate borrowed his phone to call her office and prepared to leave for the grocery store. Cecil James walked to the head of the stairs with her.

"You know more about this than I do," he said quietly. "Do you think it's foul play?"

Kate was startled. After the sheriff had accepted the hospital's diagnosis of heart failure, she was prepared to tell herself, a touch unwillingly, that it had to be from natural causes. But she kept being uncertain.

"Does Nora think that?" she asked.

He nodded. "Mr. Herren said she is convinced. That snake in his room brought on the first heart attack. Can you think of anything that might have brought on the last one?"

Kate shook her head. But suddenly she had an idea. Ash Olsen and his "mocs." Where did he get them? He was at the landing strip where Phil fell. She had assumed that he had picked them up in the marsh beyond the landing field and had reached the spot where Phil fell only after his body was moved. That's what the old man led her to believe, and the old man could have been misleading her.

Kate hurried through grocery shopping, buying heavily for the expected funeralgoers, and when everything was loaded in the boat, with the help of redheaded Bert, who was still fishing, she pulled out the chart the Nobles kept under the dash and looked at the west end of Ila Island.

The island was visible from where she stood, but the sandbars and the sunken boats were not. The sandbars shifted regularly. No matter how strictly the Coast Guard ruled about the removal of sunken hulls, many remained on the bottom of the sound, and there was an area over near the island where an old ship had sunk during a storm a century ago. It was submerged most of the year, but she and Benjy had seen it when a storm washed the sand away from it and left it temporarily exposed. But tides covered it again and she had no idea of running the Nobles' boat into it.

She had picked her course and was preparing to start the motor when young Bert handed her a plastic bag.

"Flounder," he said. "I want Mrs. Noble to have it."

"Oh, bless you, Bert," Kate said. "I'll broil it for her supper when she comes home tomorrow." She tucked it into the boat's ice chest, now empty of ice but cold enough on a winter day to keep the fish fresh for as long as it took to get her back to the island. And it was going to take a while because she intended going to see Ash Olsen.

The sun was getting low when Kate saw Ash's tall white dunes and slowed the boat to make the turn around the end of the island. Sand spits ran out from the beach like rosy fingers and Kate let the engine idle while she searched the slope of snowy sand, now golden in the light of the lowering sun, for an anchorage. She didn't want to beach the boat unless she could be sure to have a rising tide to help her launch it by herself. There must be a spot where she could safely anchor it and wade ashore. This end of the island was famous for sharks and although she had never seen one, when she and Benjy fished there she always searched the waters carefully before she went overboard.

The water was calm enough and warm, compared to the outside air, and she nosed the boat shoreward, keeping it in two or three feet of water before she threw the anchor over and pulled off her sneakers, rolled up her jeans, and slid overboard.

Ash's shack was the sole survivor of half a dozen batten-board shanties occupied in the World War II years by turpentine workers. Little of the original wooden walls had stuck out the twenty-year onslaught of autumn rains and winds and the furnace of summer sun. Where boards had blown off or rotted away, Ash had thriftily patched the structure with signs washed ashore and held together by lengths of bleached hawser, supplemented by plaited yellow nylon lines, also a gift from the sea. He had a walk outlined by plastic drink bottles buried neck deep in the sand, and at some point he must have salvaged some paint, because where the roof met the front wall he had written in shades of pink and blue the words JESUS SAVES.

Perhaps as an afterthought or maybe to frame the message, he had applied a lopsided bluefish, swimming ever skyward, a narrow and convoluted outline that could be an eel or a snake, and three open-faced flowers.

Kate smiled to see the colorful little house with the dark pines beyond it and the tall banks of snowy dunes behind it. Whatever the other islanders felt about Ash and his abode, he appeared to her to be a house-proud resident. And to complete the picture, the old man himself busied about a fire on a rusty grill before the door, incongruously wearing an apron over his dirty overalls.

"Ahoy, there!" Kate called as she emerged from a golden stand of sea oats and climbed the slight incline from the beach. She wanted to give Ash warning enough for him to put up any snakes he might be using for watchdogs.

Instead, the other guardian of his estate, Beauty, a crooked-winged old pelican, semaphored a greeting with his one powerful wing from his perch on a stump at the edge of the water. Ash had rescued Beauty from drowning when he was trapped and suffered a broken wing in a submerged tangle of nylon fishing line. Ash patched him up and released him, but Beauty, a singularly ugly bird, refused to leave. Like all pelicans he was generally silent, but the rush of air when he flapped his good wing was noise enough to attract Ash's attention.

Ash heard and turned from his fire with a smile.

"Hidy-do!" he called coming to meet her. "I'm proud to see you. My nose has been eetching, so I knowed company was a-coming. As luck would have it, I caught a nice amberjack this evening and I got it on to cook. You're bound to stay for supper."

"Oh, Ash, I wish I could," Kate said insincerely. "But the sun's going down and I'm not sure about the lights on Phil's boat. I'll feel better to get it back to the dock and tie it up. But I did want to see you and it seemed better to come by boat, since I was on my way back from Simolona. I'd hate to try to navigate those deep sand ruts after dark."

"Best not to," said Ash. "Walking them like I do is the

only sure way, the way the wind shifts that sand around and piles it up. Here, let me git you a cup of coffee."

He pushed a smoke-blackened coffeepot back toward the coals and went into the house to get a cup. He came back fastidiously wiping a Florida State University Gator souvenir mug on his apron. The sand and surf, which probably brought it in from some passing boat, had scoured the indomitable Gator with the football under his arm to insipid pallor.

"You worried about the grave, ain't you?" the old man asked.

Kate had forgotten about the grave, but it seemed a good reason for her visit, preliminary to her other questions.

"Well, the funeral's day after tomorrow. I don't know what time yet, but I reckon we'd better have a grave ready."

"Be there first thing in the morning," Ash said. "Sand's easy digging, but I ain't as stout as I usta be. Might take me a little time."

Kate sipped the coffee cautiously.

"Ash, about those cottonmouth moccasins you had this morning ..."

"Want to see 'em?" Ash asked eagerly.

"No, oh, no!" Kate said hastily. "But I wanted to know where you got them ... and when."

"As luck would have it," Ash said thoughtfully, "they was right at the edge of the airport." He spoke of the little grass landing strip as if it were Atlanta's Hartsfield or Washington's Dulles. "I'd been to my trap by the creek and wasn't tarnation in it. Then I seen the crowd gathered there around Phil and I decided to walk over that way and see what they was up to. On my way, there where the ditch dreens the airport, you know, I seen them mocs. Lucky I had my stick and my sack with me. I jes' scooped up them rascals and went on. Reckon they got out of my trap."

He paused and his eyes followed a flight of seagulls silhouetted against the rosy sunset sky,

"I wouldn't a took them over there if I'd seen Phil. Even in the sack he was a-feared of snakes. But by the time I got there—" he gulped, "didn't make no difference nohow. He was past caring, past all the evils and torments of this here life."

"Yes," Kate said sadly, watching the distant specks the gulls had become. She stood up and surreptitiously tipped her coffee into the sand. "Ash, you said you had somebody who would buy moccasins."

The old man looked uncomfortable. He poked at his fire and used a peeled myrtle stick to turn his fish.

"A feller," he said hesitantly, "buys 'em to ship to some museum or laboratory place, or someplace like that. You know they pay good money?"

"Have you delivered them?" And then the important question. "Who is this man?"

"You know, I fergit his name," Ash said, chuckling in self-deprecation. "You know I never was no good with names."

"Ash, tell me the truth," Kate said sternly. "Who wanted you to get those snakes?"

"That feller—I cain't think of his name—ships marine stuff to some laboratory somers." He brightened. "He ain't came for them yet, Kate. They still on hand. Think I should git rid of them?"

"It's your merchandise, Ash. Do whatever you think best. I just wonder if somebody used your snakes to bring on Phil's heart attack. That rattlesnake in his house last week ... who put that there? Did your customer buy that one?"

"Oh, no," said Ash. "Not him. He only wants water things. Marine life, so to speak."

They both were silent for a moment and Ash swallowed hard and said suddenly, "Kate, you don't think I'd put a snake in Phil's house, do you?"

"Not you, Ash. But somebody did."

She glanced at the sky, which was ominously graying in the east. A loon cried in the pine woods and Kate listened instinctively for its mate to answer.

"Do they still nest by the old shell mound?" she asked.

Ash's head seemed to bobble, neither nodding in the affirmative or shaking in the negative, and Kate remembered that the old man, like so many old-timers in the area, was superstitious about the shell mound.

Archaeological crews from the university had long ago determined that it was not a burial ground but simply a midden of oyster shells piled there by Indians during their autumnal returnings to feast. Ash, brave about snakes, gave it a wide berth but, oddly enough, never repeated the stories mullet fishermen told of seeing ghosts there on moonlit nights.

Suddenly the old man drew himself up and said peremptorily, "Let's have a word of prayer."

Kate started to demur. Twilight was descending and she felt a need to hurry. Besides, she'd thought Ash reserved his praying and preaching for the unfriendly game warden.

He had already lifted his right hand and rolled his eyes back under the wispy white brush of his brow

"O Lord!" he cried. "Thou has searched me out and knowed me. Thou knowest my down-sitting and my uprising. Thou understandest my thought. If I had aught to do with the passing of thy servant, Phil, O Lord, strike me dead and feed me to the sharks. Amen."

"Amen," Kate echoed automatically.

Ash followed her down to the boat and waded out in the shallow water to give it a push toward the channel as she cranked it up.

The sun was gone, but its afterglow spread a mantle of golden light over the island, and Kate, hugging the shore, felt the old rush of joy, long missing, sweep over her at its beauty. The water, pale green near the beach, deepened into lapis lazuli farther out. The chilly wind she had felt on Ash's point had slacked off and the bay was silken smooth except where a ripple of foam edged the waves on the beach with white lace.

She passed her own house and slowed the motor to study it. Nestled back of dunes and banks of cedar and wild rosemary with pines framing it, only the rooftop and upper half of the screened front porch showed. The cedar and cypress siding had weathered a soft dove gray, just what she and Benjy had hoped for when they rejected the new aluminum siding which had hit the island and was the alternative. Newer houses in

Mediterranean shades of blue and rose were pretty, salt and sun resistant, but they did not meld into the landscape the way the old unpainted ones did, and Kate was glad of hers and eager to tie up Phil's boat and get back to it.

As she rounded the point which sheltered the little boat basin, she saw a dozen or more people on the dock. A sailboat she didn't recognize was anchored a little distance from the dock and two or three brightly painted powerboats, not there when she left, had arrived and were tied up. The *Lily Belle*, the old ferryboat which came to the island only on weekends, wallowed comfortably in the little waves Kate's arrival had churned up. Its captain, Raynor Ellis, walked down the little wharf to meet her and reach for the line she prepared to throw out.

She smiled her thanks and accepted the hand he extended to help her step up to the wharf from the bow.

"Thank you, Captain Ellis," she said.

"You're welcome, Mrs. Mulcay," he replied with a show of white teeth against his sun-browned face. And then gravely, "We're so sorry. All of us were just saying losing Philip Noble is a disaster to this island."

"And a very personal disaster," a woman who walked up behind him said.

"Mindy!" Kate cried, ducking around Ellis and walking into the embrace of a very tall woman with her white hair tied into a chignon and her slender body enveloped in a knee-length fisherman's sweater, which met high red leather boots. "Mindy! I'm so glad you're here!"

Melinda Mason was in her seventies and still dominant in matters political and philanthropic in northwest Florida. A famous beauty and Tallahassee debutante, she had been a frivolous fritterer "from cornpone country to Cannes," she often said, until the civil rights movement flared in other parts of the country and, as she happily proclaimed, she "freed my slaves and went to march in Selma and ride buses in Montgomery."

She had never married. A prince from some little European country had courted her on three continents, but when he found out she was broke, he lost interest.

"It didn't devastate me to lose him," she told friends. "But when I had to sell my plane, I cried for a week."

Mindy had first come to the island with a fly-in of Ninety-Nines, the organization Amelia Earhart had started when there were only ninety-nine licensed women pilots in the country. Mindy had been one of them, a winner in the Powder Puff Derby's cross-country speed races and a friend of Jacqueline Cochran, who had risen from an impoverished west Florida mill village to become a wealthy cosmetician and a founder of World War II's invincible WASPS. The day the fly-in brought her and her friends to Ila Island, Mindy picnicked on the white beach, swam naked in the blue surf, and made up her mind to have a cottage there.

Her sleek, shining little Bonanza Beechcraft came regularly to the grass strips for years. When she had used up the Mason fortune, she sold the plane and bought a boat, which she piloted across the sound looking as she stood in the bow like a figurehead on a Viking bark, slender and elegant in tailored slacks, her white hair flying, her black eyes alight with excitement.

"Mindy, you drive too fast," Philip Noble had told her often.

"Aw, Philip," Melinda would say, kissing him on the cheek, "I'm just doing what Winnie Churchill advised. 'Mindy, my child,' he said, 'live audaciously!'"

"Just so you live," Phil would grumble.

Now Phil was not living and Mindy Mason, no longer able to maintain a boat of her own and reduced to adjusting her comings and goings to the weekend ferry schedule, stood beside his boat, noticeably stricken to have lost her friend.

Other members of the group gathered around, leaving on the dock the coolers and canvas bags and boxes of groceries which constituted the tatty baggage of weekenders. A couple had their dogs leashed to the ferry dock railing and Kate, remembering Pepper left behind in the cottage, hurried to collect young Bert's flounder gift to Nora and her groceries and move toward her car.

Raynor Ellis was the handsomest man Kate thought she had ever seen, standing even taller than Mindy's six feet, with bright yellow hair pushing out around his red baseball cap and his sea-green eyes fringed by extravagantly long, thick lashes. Now he took Mindy's arm and edged the group toward the shore so Kate could get by.

"Funeral's day after tomorrow, folks," he said. "The *Lily Belle* will bring over friends and relatives at noon. Cecil James is going to bring the coffin in his boat."

"Everybody come to my house afterward," Mindy said. "We'll have some food."

Kate stowed her groceries in the car and stood a

moment watching the new arrivals disperse to their cars and go through the islander's moment of suspense about what neglect and salt air had done to vehicles since they parked them there. Would they start or wouldn't they?

Several of them waved and Mindy and the ferryboat captain, who had had no trouble starting her Jeep station wagon, pulled up beside Kate's car.

"You make it all right?" Ray asked.

"I think so," said Kate. "It started this morning."

"Phil," said Mindy briefly.

"I know," Kate said. "He hated to see any machine abused and neglected and he really did look after this old car all the months I wasn't here."

"Want to come and have a drink and a sandwich with us?" Mindy asked.

Kate shook her head. "No, thank you. I'm going to check Nora's house and then I better get to mine and see about my dog. I'm tired," she confessed ruefully.

"Then I'll see you in the morning," Mindy said. "We can do up the chapel and see about the cemetery."

"Ash is going to dig the grave," Kate said.

Ellis laughed shortly. "Better check that out," he said.

Kate watched them drive away, feeling obscurely irritated.

Raynor Ellis had gibed at Ash and, of the two, Kate thought she liked Ash better. She wondered about the ferryboat captain and Mindy. The thirty- or forty-year difference in their ages hardly seemed a consideration when she saw them together—both tall, slender, suntanned, and gorgeous.

Kate wondered where Mindy kept her age, because it certainly hadn't surfaced on her face or figure. Her fine-boned face was smooth and satiny, her body that of a dancer.

The bond between them may have been aviation. Before he came to Simolona, Ray had been an airline pilot. He had his own boat, a trim seagoing launch which he kept tied up by the ferryboat pier in Simolona. Kate had heard that he lived on it more than he lived in a small apartment he had in an old house across the river. She and Benjy had drinks on it once and had been greatly impressed by its amenities—bed, stove, head. They had wondered a bit about his income. The job of skipper of the *Lily Belle* didn't pay a princely sum; but then, he apparently had no family to support. At least no wife or children had appeared on the scene in the two or three years Raynor had been there.

She thought of the gathering at the dock and tried to fit names to faces, difficult because some of the people were newcomers she seldom saw. She had similar difficulty with the group of men who had gathered around Phil at the landing strip that morning. In the shock of his death and the arrival of the helicopter, followed by Ash and his "mocs," she had failed to notice who was there. Except Greg Herren, of course, who made his presence felt by taking charge. In any case, she was too tired to sort it all out now, she thought as she drove the little distance to Nora's house on the gulf.

The Nobles' house seemed in order and quiet at first. But suddenly a deep voice startled Kate and she started to back out of the kitchen door.

Somebody was in there!

She was about to call out and then was relieved that she hadn't been that kind of fool. It was Phil's marine radio on his desk in the living room. He kept it on to monitor activity on the sound and the waters of the gulf as far as it would reach. There had been times when Phil had the first report of boats in difficulty in the gulf and had relayed their location to the marine patrol on shore. The Coast Guard was too far away in Panama City or Pensacola to get to a small boat in the gulf in a hurry and if the Marine Patrol was not available, Phil took his own boat or borrowed a bigger one from a neighbor and went to the rescue.

Oh, Phil, Kate thought, moving to the living room door, *we need you.*

The ruby eye of the radio was the only light in the room, but beyond the windows the waters of the gulf were a silver shimmer.

Kate stood and listened a moment. A shrimp boat captain was exchanging greetings with another shrimp boat captain and reporting the presence of a barge aground on a sandbar in the sound. It would remain there until the next high tide, probably all night, and it was well for the small fishing smacks to look for its lights.

Relieved, Kate returned to the kitchen and went out the back door, leaving a light on in case Nora came home sooner than she had planned.

Several houses on the gulf side were lit up. Their owners had come on the ferry. One or two showed activity on the sound side. Dr. Wells, the marine biologist from the university, had apparently arrived. Jim Preston, the retired forest ranger, and his wife, Emmy, had lights on. Mary Darden, the Apalachicola social worker, was not here now, but she lived close enough to come on the day of the funeral. Deb and Dab Winkler—who knew where they were? Probably at the other end of the world and had not been notified. Their little house was dark.

Her own house was also dark. Pepper came out from under it to meet her.

"What are you doing outside?" she demanded as she unloaded the grocery boxes. "Did you push that screen door open?"

As she climbed the steps with Pepper at her heels, she knew he had not. They had scolded him enough about pawing at the screens to deter him, she hoped. Besides, that door frame, swelled by rains, stuck at the bottom. Pepper would not have been able to open it without help, and she couldn't think of a neighbor who, finding him confined to the porch and her absent, would have let him out.

Nothing in the house seemed disturbed. She walked around turning on lights and looking at her and Benjy's possessions, none of much value but lovingly acquired and arranged through the years. A shell-framed mirror, a primitive, hand-carved pine duck decoy, a fish-shaped tureen to hold chowder, books, and small pieces of drift-wood and pottery. She put up the groceries and got out a can of food for Pepper, who unexpectedly whimpered and pawed at his head.

"What ails you, boy?" Kate asked cheerfully, and then she saw him in the light.

There were cuts around his head and across his ears.

"Oh, Pepper," Kate cried, kneeling. "What happened to you? How on earth did you get cut up like this?"

It was not easy to tell how deep the cuts were because they were covered with congealed and dried blood. Kate got a pan of warm water and a bar of soap and sat on the floor with Pepper's head in her lap, mopping at the cuts until they were clean and visible. They did not appear to be deep, but she worried that one or two of them might open up and bleed, and she held those together with small pieces of bandage and tape, hoping that Pepper wouldn't try to paw them off. Others she painted with iodine, and then she gave the dog an aspirin wrapped up in a bit of ground beef.

"You're a good fellow," she said, in praise of the docility with which he received treatment of his wounds. She looked him over carefully and to her surprise saw that his feet and legs were covered with dried mud.

"Now, where did you get that?" she demanded. "There's no mud around here—just sand!"

Pepper thumped his tail conversationally and looked at the package of hamburger on the counter.

"Okay," said Kate. "You've had a hard day. You are welcome to my supper. I'm not hungry, anyhow."

She wasn't. She sat on the front porch and looked at the lights of the grounded barge across the sound and worried. Pepper's wounds had to have been deliberately inflicted. But who would do such a thing? And why? He was a peaceable dog. He never even growled at anybody unless they appeared to be a threat to Kate. He would have slept in the shade on the screened porch all afternoon and only barked at strangers who approached the house.

The night had turned warm and Kate would ordinarily have left the French doors leading to the screened front porch open. She liked to hear the waves and smell the salt breeze. She drew companionship from watching from her bed the shrimp boats in the sound, looking in the distance like small jeweled pins with their rigging outlined in lights.

Tonight she closed and locked all the doors and invited Pepper to her room to sleep on a beach towel beside her bed.

Mindy was already at the island's small weathered chapel when Kate, with Pepper beside her, arrived with brooms and polish and window cleaner.

The little church had been a post–World War II gift to the island from the parents of two brothers who had trained in landing craft on Ila and subsequently died in the Normandy invasion. They understood that few of the island colony cared about going to church, but their sons had a spiritual awakening when they trained there, not through any outside help from the few families who could get there for weekends and summer stays, but because of the beauty and tranquility of the place. They had found a peace of spirit and had not feared death, they wrote their parents.

It was the only memorial the bereaved couple could think of and since they didn't have much money it was blessedly simple and small. The exterior walls were weathered cypress, the interior white-painted pine paneling. A small pulpit and twenty plain wooden pews furnished the little sanctuary. The donors had wanted to provide stained-glass windows, but Nora and Phil persuaded them that the view through clear glass windows was what their sons had loved and it would be inspiring to worshipers. The little building stood on a solid phalanx of dunes facing the gulf, directly opposite the harbor. It was visible to all comers and always open to those who wanted to visit it, but Kate had an idea few did. Only occasionally, when somebody's weekend guest happened to be a minister, did they have services there, and those were scantily attended. However, the islanders had chipped in and bought a bell—an old sailing ship's bell—and installed it in a frame by the front door. It was tolled in time of trouble, a shipwreck or a fire, and islanders seemed to have pride in and affection for what they named the Brothers' Chapel.

Mindy sat on the front steps, hugging her knees in their designer jeans and looking out to sea. She arose to meet Kate and Pepper and eyed the basket of cleaning materials approvingly.

"I came to help clean, but I forgot all that," she said. "I'll make up for it by sweeping."

"No need to," said Kate. "It's not that big a job. Why don't we cut some greenery and you can decorate while I clean?"

The idea pleased Mindy and in a little while the chapel gleamed under their ministrations, fragrant with beeswax and garlands of swamp myrtle and pine. The windows sparkled and were open to let the winds from the gulf sweep out any fugitive wasps or musty smells.

Kate put the cleaning gear in her car and headed for the dock to pick up Nora at Simolona. She met Ash coming up the road with a shovel on his shoulder. She did not think Ash had been to her house and abused Pepper, but she was relieved when Pepper, still sore and limping a little, walked up to the old man, wagging his tail.

Nora and Greg Herren arrived in Simolona before she did and waited on one of the benches at dockside. Nora was very pale and huddled into a borrowed jacket as if the wind from the sound were attacking her. *It's not that cold*, Kate was thinking. *She must be ill.* She poked around in the bow where the life jackets were and came out with one for Nora and a plastic tarp of the kind carried by Phil and most boat owners for emergency use in case of a breakdown on a winter day.

Nora accepted both and smiled gratefully as she wound the plastic tarp around her chest and shoulders.

"I've been so c-c-cold," she said. "I can't seem to get warm."

Kate hugged her.

"You come on to my house and I'll give you something hot to drink and tuck you in bed," she said.

"Ah, no," whispered Nora. "I'll go home. I have to, sooner or later."

Kate settled Nora where the windshield would protect her from most of the wind and all the spray and turned to the driver's seat. Greg Herren was already there.

"I'll take her across," he said.

Kate looked at Nora, but she was looking out over the marsh, uninterested.

Kate sat in the back thinking sarcastically, *You probably think a woman can't run a boat as well as you can, masterful one!*

She was positive that she knew the channel markers and the sandbars better than any Johnny-Come-Lately from Wisconsin, but it was Nora's boat, and if she acquiesced, who was Kate to argue?

Laughing gulls were all over the harbor, swooping down to the surface of the water and soaring skyward. They were so beautiful, Kate thought. All impeccable white bodies and velvety black heads, but their maniacal "Ha! Ha! Ha!" sounded more mocking than usual today. She looked at Nora, who was listless and oblivious to her surroundings and encased in plastic, and even Pepper, always eager to stand in the bow of the boat like a figurehead, was slumped on the deck, sore of body and quenched of spirit.

Greg Herren did handle the boat expertly, slowing to no-wake speed as they approached the Ila dock, steering around the boats already moored there and snugging her up to the Nobles' mooring.

Unencumbered for once by luggage and groceries, the three of them climbed out slowly. Kate helped Nora to unwind the tarp and she folded it and put it back in the niche under the bow. Nora stood waiting for her.

"I think I will go home with you," she said quietly.

"Good," said Kate. "I'll build a fire and cook your young friend Bert's flounder for our lunch. He's a nice boy, Nora, and so fond of you and Phil."

Nora nodded, her eyes brimming.

Kate did build the fire in the fireplace and gave Nora a glass of sherry to sip while she set the table, put together a salad, and heated rolls to go with the floun- der, which waited, seasoned and buttered, under the broiler.

Nora tried valiantly to eat and to make conversation, but her head drooped and her eyes closed and finally she gave up and went to the guest room, where Kate had laid out a flannel nightgown for her.

"I want to talk about it," she said haltingly as Kate pulled up one of her old handmade quilts to cover her. "But I can't yet. Too tired."

"Never mind," said Kate, leaning over to kiss her forehead. "Talk'll keep until you've rested awhile."

She wondered as she cleared the table and put the plates in the dishwasher if talk would keep. She had a strong feeling that something hovered over the island, their beloved Ila Island.

5

►Cecil James's launch arrived midmorning with two undertaker's men to unload the coffin containing Phil's body. They rolled it up the sand and shell road to the Brothers' Chapel, where the pulpit had to be moved to make room for it.

Nora, with Mindy and Kate beside her, followed it and sat for a while in one of the old pine pews, her head bowed.

The *Lily Belle* arrived with a full load of friends from Simolona and Tallahassee. The governor had sent a representative and there were department heads who had worked with the Nobles on environmental issues and knew Phil as a fighter to save the barrier islands from exploitation. Redheaded Bert, shy and alone, came. The editor of the Simolona weekly, the *Beacon*, was there and Doc Joe, the druggist, had brought his own minister, the pastor of the Methodist church.

"I didn't know if Nora would need him or if she had asked somebody else," he confided to Kate, "but he's a nice fellow and won't mind if he's not asked to officiate. I just felt that at a time like this you can't have too many preachers."

"You're right," Kate said. "I'm not sure Nora thought of that. She seems to be in a state of shock."

"Well, Reverunt Henry knew Phil. They worked together for the crippled children's hospital," Doc Joe said. "He wanted to come and he'll do the service unless Nora has made other arrangements."

Nora had apparently made no arrangements. Normally a poised and confident woman who would go out to meet their friends with grace and gratitude, she was silent and detached, hardly listening to expressions of sympathy, allowing Kate and Mindy to guide her to the front bench in the chapel, where she sat staring at the pine coffin and the American flag which covered it. Somebody, remembering Phil's wartime service in the Air Force, had thought to provide it.

The chapel filled and overflowed to the sand dune outside, where a dozen people stood looking in through the open windows. When the funeralgoers were settled, the chapel was quiet except for the sound of breakers on the beach. Moments elapsed and finally Mindy, uneasy with the silence, turned and nodded toward the young minister.

Standing beside the coffin, he produced a prayerbook from his pocket and read the simple beautiful service for the dead, ending with the prayer that Philip Noble had gone to a place of refreshment, light, and peace.

The undertaker's men came forward and rolled the

coffin down the center aisle to the door. Kate knew Nora was supposed to follow it, but she didn't stir for long moments. When she did move, she stumbled on the rough pine floor, looking blindly after her husband's coffin.

Mindy took charge of her.

The congregation waited its turn and then awkwardly filed out. Mindy took a firm grip on Nora's arm, holding her back. When the visitors were outside, she faced Nora and said sternly, "Listen to me. You've got to hold up your head and handle this! You're acting like a wimp and Philip Noble would be ashamed of you!"

Kate gasped, but then Nora lifted her head, swallowed hard, and moved toward the door. Mindy was due an approving smile and Kate gave it to her. The older woman, slim as a teenager and elegant in a black silk dress, had faced losses and grief many times in her many years and Kate knew she had neither whimpered nor bowed to adversity.

Restless storm winds had piled sand on the narrow shell path to the little graveyard up in the pine grove, and for a time it appeared that the carriage carrying the coffin would be stuck. But half a dozen men joined the professionals and pushed it out.

A picket fence, grayed by time and the weather, enclosed the small burying ground. An unknown ship's carpenter had carved from heart pine some of the markers on the graves, ornamenting them with crosses, and one—a child's grave, from the size of it—had a rough approximation of a lamb. Names were overgrown with lichens and impossible to read, but Kate knew from Phil that some of the graves were those of early mariners whose sailing ships were wrecked on the island or were lost at sea. There were no marble or granite tombstones, but shells covered the sand mounds. There was a new limestone pillar near the gate, but no grave beside it. Kate paused to read the inscription:

SARAH LANGHORNE, 19. GONE BUT NOT FORGOTTEN

That was the girl, Nora had told her, who had waded out into the cut and was never seen again. It was accepted as suicide, but Nora did not believe that. Odd that there should be a monument to her on the island, since she had only been visiting.

Kate hurried to catch up with Nora and Mindy, who stood by the open hole Ash had dug and waited for the minister to speak.

He came to the part about "ashes to ashes, dust to dust" and scooped up a handful of the gleaming white sand which owed its silvery content to the quartz which makes up so much of the gulf beach sand. *Neither ashes nor dust,* Kate thought, *but a magical element Philip would be pleased to return to.*

The service was over and the minister folded the flag and presented it to Nora. Ash, dressed in an odd combination of blue serge trousers and khaki Army tunic with a spotted tie, had been standing with his shovel under a pine tree at a little distance.

The undertaker's men had started to fill the grave, but the old man interrupted.

"Jesta minute, fellers," he said. "He was my friend. I want to do it."

He looked imploringly at Nora and she nodded.

"Thank you, Ash. I'd like that."

Surprised, the professionals withdrew and presently followed the rest of the mourners down the hill to the beach and Mindy's house.

Mindy, born rich and imperishably fastidious, had not felt it necessary to have a luxurious carpeted, air-conditioned beach house like those that were going up along the coast from Mobile to Miami. Hers was a weathered, drafty old barn with the wind sweeping through and unpainted board floors which drifting sand had polished. The furniture was makeshift or hand-me-downs—an old door on sawhorses for a table on the porch, wicker divans with shabby, faded sailcloth cushions, the old Brumby rockers acquired when split white oak was used to bottom them before varnish and cane took over. She had bowed to convenience and installed a bathroom, although the original privy was still there, leaning into the wind.

An old-fashioned wood range dominated the kitchen and sent out warmth to welcome the funeralgoers coming in out of the wind. Shelves overflowed with books and one corner housed music and tapes.

Mindy had spread a cloth on the long table in the living room, centered it with an arrangement of red-berried yaupon, and set out smoked turkey and home-made rolls, shrimp and vegetable dips. Doc Joe sent Bert to the dock to bring up a case of soft drinks he had brought. Mary Darden, the plump sweet-faced social worker, arrived with a vegetable casserole. Emmy Preston brought a basket full of cookies. Kate's own contribution was an assortment of relishes, salted pecans, and a platter of chicken she had fried at dawn. Dr. Wells, the biologist, walked back to his plane and brought up a gallon of fresh oysters, bought off a boat at Apalachicola that morning.

Kate hurried to the pantry to get little dishes to hold the horseradish sauce and bumped into Mindy and Ray Ellis in close conversation.

"Bourbon and scotch and some wines," Mindy said hastily, and Kate had the idea that had not been what they were talking about at all.

"Right," said Ray, and then grinned at Kate. "I've just been appointed bartender."

He collected glasses and plastic cups and returned to the living room. Mindy turned her back on Kate and reached for the little sauce dishes. Kate thought the back of her neck seemed unnaturally pink, but she couldn't be sure.

Finally they all stood around eating and drinking and Kate looked them over carefully. Almost the entire island population was there. The young Winklers had flown in from some south Florida or Caribbean playground during the night and they cornered Kate to ask details of Phil's death.

Both small and blond and tanned a uniformly rich bronze by resort suns, they might have been brother and sister—almost identical twins—as they stood, arms linked, leaning together listening to Kate's words. They even wore look-alike white duck trousers and middies.

"One heart attack and he seemed to recover and then he had another—out by the landing strip," Kate was saying.

Nora appeared at her side.

"He was killed," she said clearly.

Several people turned to listen.

"Oh, no!" squeaked Deb. "Not Phil! Everybody loved Phil! Dabney and I don't even want to come to the island without him."

"That's right," said Dab.

"That's right," somebody in the group echoed, and several other voices assented.

Nora's laugh was bitter. "Then it will be a deserted island and that will make it easy for some fat corporation to pick it up cheap!"

She turned back to the table and put down her glass. "I don't care what happens to Ila now. Without Phil it doesn't matter to me. But I mean to find out who killed him!"

Greg Herren was by her side in an instant

"Come, dear, you're chilly in that light suit. Let's stand by that great old stove I saw in the kitchen."

He has no business patronizing Nora, Kate thought as Nora let Herren steer her from the room. *Besides, she is not wearing a "light" suit but one of my good wool ones.* Kate, remembering how cold Nora had been, had pulled it out of her cedar closet and pressed it for Nora to wear to the funeral. *If anything, Nora's hot today.*

She returned her attention to the young Winklers, who still stood before her looking stunned.

"Was Phil really killed?" gasped Deb. "Why did Nora say that?"

"Oh, she's just upset," Dab said comfortably.

"Well, granting that she's upset, it's not impossible that somebody did something to cause Phil's heart attacks," Kate surprised herself by saying.

"Like Sarah Langhorne," put in Mary Darden, joining them. "That girl interned with me. She was going to make an excellent social worker. She was young and pretty, with only two more years in college. You'll never make me believe that she went to the cut by herself way down there near that crazy old man's shack and deliberately walked out into that racing tide and drowned herself."

Around the table people had stopped eating and stood, drinks in hand, looking troubled.

"Sarah was staying at our house at the time," Emmy Preston said. "She came a lot with our Emaline. Jim and I weren't here, but Emaline brought her and left her for a few days. We got the impression that she was happy. She had a lot of studying to do and, of course, it was too chilly in December for her to swim anywhere, much less at the cut. We always warned the girls not to swim alone."

"Do you suppose that eccentric old fellow had something to do with it?" the young minister asked.

"You mean Ash?" asked Kate. "No! Ash wouldn't hurt anybody."

"Absolutely not!" put in Mindy. And then, glancing around at her guests, she said, "Everybody eat. All this food ... has everybody plates? Kate, Ray made a Bloody

Mary the way you like it, all zipped up with Tabasco. Come!"

She towed Deb and Dab off with them to the improvised bar and whispered to Doc Joe to divert the conversation from violent death. The old gentleman was glad enough to talk about his own problems, the end of the famous and well-loved soda fountain in his drugstore.

But Kate's mind was on Sarah Langhorne, a girl she had never known. She took her drink from Raynor Ellis, who was even more handsome without his ferryboat captain's cap. She didn't remember ever having seen him bareheaded. And his shock of golden hair, brushed into a kind of gleaming pompadour, belonged on a Nordic movie star.

He smiled as he handed her the tall Bloody Mary, and Kate thought his white teeth went with the rest of him—flawless, too good for everyday local consumption. He needed to be a star.

"I hope I haven't overdone the Tabasco," he said to Kate. "Mindy said you like it hot."

"I'm sure it's fine," said Kate, but it was blisteringly hot and after a sip or two she eased it to a table and moved over to talk to Emmy Preston.

"That marker in the graveyard ..." she began.

"Sarah's parents," Emmy intercepted. "She was their only child and they seem to take it particularly hard that her body was never found. I reckon there's some kind of comfort in having a body and a grave in a known spot."

Kate nodded. "I know. Like soldiers brought home from the battlefield."

Emmy looked down at her glass of wine and raised bright inquisitive eyes to Kate's face.

"You think Sarah was a victim—like on a battle-field?"

"I haven't any idea," Kate said. "I was just interested in the marker. Isn't it kind of unusual to have a stone like that without a grave?"

"I don't know," said Emmy, "but I sympathize with Sarah's parents. They live up in Georgia in Waycross, but they've come several times and put flowers there and I think they want all of us to remember their daughter and that she was here."

People were beginning to depart when Ash appeared at the back door, shovel over his shoulder. He saw Mindy saying good-bye to a group and he waited for her attention.

"I'm done," he said. "Heaped it up nice and round and put the prettiest shells I got on it, couple of conchs and a lot of king's crowns and double sunrises. Phil liked them king's crowns. Had to git 'em on the flats on the bay side."

Nora came up in time to overhear him.

"God bless you, Ash," she said, and leaned over and kissed the old man on the forehead. "You always do the right thing."

Raynor Ellis winced involuntarily as if the idea of a kiss on that pocked and permanently smoke-blackened face was thoroughly repugnant to him. But he managed to smile when Mindy said warmly, "Ash does do the right thing and we all thank you, sir. Now come and have something to eat."

"Well, if I ain't gon' mar up your party," Ash said, putting down his shovel.

Raynor left to load up the ferry. Nora decided to go home and spend a little time alone.

"I'll show up if I find it too hard," she said to Kate.

Kate lingered to help Mindy clear away and fill a plate and set it before Ash at the kitchen table. Mindy got down a basket and filled it with leftover food for the old man to take back with him. While Mindy was in the living room putting away the bottles of whiskey, Ash stopped chewing and wiped his mouth with the back of his hand.

"Kate," he said diffidently, "I ain't always done things right. I wish Nora hadn't of said that."

"Oh, Ash, that's true of everybody. None of us is right all the time. In fact, some of us"—she managed a smile—"are hardly ever right."

The old man sighed and looked around the warm plain kitchen distractedly.

"It ain't that," he said. "Not ordinary rightness. I done a wrong."

Kate stopped in the middle of the kitchen with a plate in her hand. There was urgency in his voice. He had something he wanted to tell.

"What is it, Ash?" she asked gently. "You want to tell me about it?"

His old eyes fell on Mindy coming in from the other room and he shook his head and returned his attention to the food.

Kate hovered around the stove wishing she could think of an errand to get rid of Mindy, but the older woman was plainly exhausted by the day's demands and she pulled up the rocker which stood by the window and collapsed in it.

"Nice to have heat," she murmured. "I think it's turning cold."

Suddenly Kate thought of driving Ash back down the island.

"Ash, you must be worn out from all that shoveling," she said. "And the wind is freshening. I'll drive you home."

He shook his head. "No, ma'am. I come in my boat. I aim to go in my boat and throw the cast net a few times."

"You might as well let him alone, Kate," Mindy said. "Ash is going to do as he pleases and there are days when I believe he hates human society."

Ash guffawed.

"You right, Miss Mindy. You must know how it is to be crowded and cornered."

"Of course," Mindy said.

"Well," said Kate, looking around for her jacket and her purse, "if you all feel that way about human society, I guess I'll take this portion of it on down the beach. Mindy, it was nice. I know Nora appreciated it and I think seeing everybody helped her."

She collected Pepper, who was dozing luxuriously in a lounge on Mindy's porch.

"How about it, Kate?" Mindy asked as she went by to the door. "Did you get any ideas about what happened to Phil? Are you going to work on this case?"

Kate paused. "Case? I don't know. I haven't thought about it."

6

►The western sky over the mainland was smeared
with saffron and carmine as Kate's old car
wheezed and galumphed down the beach road. The gulf
seemed drained of color and the waves, deep blue and
white-edged earlier, were sullen gray rollers. A thunder-
storm was shaping up, Kate decided, and tried to hurry.
A real blow from the north or the west would sweep
through her French doors, drenching everything.

The rain hit as she drove in the yard and let Pepper
out of the backseat. Pepper did not dash for the dunes
or the beach, as was his custom, but followed Kate
indoors, docile, limping a little.

Worries, personal variety, Kate thought, watching
him. *I can't take on a "case." A wild cat in the house could
have been an accident, but somebody deliberately hurt my
dog—and why? Why any of it?*

She had some experience working on cases with the
Atlanta Police Department, especially as long as her
husband, a homicide detective, lived. There you had the

benefit of the experts—fingerprints and footprints and all the forensics authority of a big state crime lab. There were lineups of suspects from which you could often pluck the killer. But the lineup here ... she thought of the friends and neighbors gathered around Mindy's table. Good-looking, well-dressed people with agreeable manners and no possible motive for murder or even the cruel mischief she had been subjected to.

Kate checked anxiously for signs of new mischief in her house and, seeing none, applied herself to closing windows and doors.

What she expected would be a minor squall turned into a full-fledged electrical storm. Thunder rumbled and crashed, lightning exploded over the island, taking with it the island's electric current. Without lights it was too dark in the cottage to read. Pepper, terrified of thunder and lightning, whimpered and huddled close to her chair.

The generators which provided electricity to the islanders were capricious. Like Pepper, Kate thought: terrified of thunder and lightning. They often quit before the heavy artillery of a storm. Islanders were philosophical about it, lighting candles and kerosene lamps, bringing out campstoves and being careful not to open their refrigerators or use their toilets until water pumps were working again.

Kate sat on in the twilight watching the storm-lashed waves on the beach and listening to the beat of the rain on her tin roof. She thought of Ash setting out in his leaky old skiff, propelled only by a pair of oars and his own strength. Once somebody, probably a tourist, feeling sorry for the old man, had given him an outboard motor. Ash had accepted it with every appearance of gratitude, but the donor was no more than halfway to the mainland on the ferryboat when the motor mysteriously lurched off the stern of Ash's boat and disappeared overboard and Ash contentedly resumed rowing.

He couldn't make it in this storm, Kate worried. Waves in the sound were high enough and rough enough to capsize him and lightning could strike him. She walked to the door and saw nothing but grayness. She walked back to the radio on the refrigerator. It was silent, of course, its red eye blind. But there were batteries to power it and all she had to do was find the proper switch.

She fiddled with the contraption, wishing for Benjy, who loved it and took pleasure in talking to island friends and fishing boat skippers at sea. Suddenly there was a lull in the rain. Kate waited, tense, listening. In the time of autumn hurricanes that lull, that sudden ominous quiet, was fearful, literally the lull before the full ferocity of the storm. But in January ... Abruptly the whole sky seemed on fire, suffused with red, and then a crash shook the house like a sonic boom.

Pepper whined in alarm and pushed against her knees. The radio rattled to life and Jim Preston's voice shouted, "Fire! Fire on the island! Something near the dock has been hit!"

Kate grabbed an oilskin poncho off a hook by the back door and ran for her car. Fire was the ultimate horror for islanders. They had no help from the mainland ten miles away and the rusty Army surplus pumper they kept in a shed near the dock might start and it might not, might have a full tank of water and might be dry. Anything metal was subject to leaks, and the tank might not have been checked in months. To have houses, cars, boats burned would be disaster enough, but if fire got loose in the woods, it would be a conflagration that would burn for days with all those big turpentine trees, with their raw resin faces, ignited like torches. The little island would be burned to a crisp and there was a good chance that its inhabitants would not escape.

The car was rain-soaked and sluggish to start, but Kate pumped the accelerator and pleaded "Please, please go!" and it choked, rallied, and obeyed.

When she got to the dock, she saw it was Nora's house. Or had been.

Nothing was standing but an old water heater tank and the blackened carcass of Nora's Jeep.

"Nora! Nora!" Kate got out of the car screaming.

"She's safe," Greg Herren, drenched and smoke-blackened, called to her from the little woodshed which stood in the backyard and miraculously seemed untouched by the fire. He had a hose in his hand—a futile gesture until the generators started working again, but the rain was falling again anyhow and would presumably wet down any sparks left in the ashes.

"Where? Where's Nora?" Kate entreated, and Emmy Preston separated herself from the group which had gathered and came to Kate.

"Mindy's," she said. "She's going to be all right. Fortunately, she was outside—down at the dock checking on the boat. She wasn't sure the pump was working and got to thinking it might sink from all that rain. She went to see and was walking back when that lightning struck. She tried to go back in the house—I guess to save things—so she suffered some from the smoke."

"I can't bear it!" Kate cried. "She's had too much."

"I guess Jim and I got here first," Emmy went on. "He heard that peculiar boom and he knew it was not just lightning but an explosion. He got on the radio hoping to get help. Did you hear him?"

Kate nodded. "I came as fast as I could."

"Everybody did," said Emmy. "But it was too late. That old house was like tinder. It went up before we could get here."

"I want to see Nora," Kate said, and turned to walk down the beach to Mindy's.

"I'll go with you," Emmy said. "There's nothing we can do here."

The thunder and lightning had ceased, but the rain poured down in a steady unrelenting deluge for which the island was famous. There were times when it rained seven inches in one day and now it seemed bent on breaking all records.

Nora and Mindy sat by the wood range in Mindy's kitchen with a kerosene lamp and candles for light against the gathering night. Nora's face was pinched with weariness and grief. Her eyebrows were gone and her soft gray hair was singed.

Kate leaned to hug her and Emmy followed suit. Mindy wore a long gray terry-cloth robe with her hair in a towel and had enveloped Nora in one of her chic wool bathrobes. Kate and Emmy divested themselves of rain gear and pulled up chairs to the kitchen stove.

"Brandies for everybody," Mindy said. "Nora needs it and the rest of us deserve it. Such a horrible, horrible thing! The island seems utterly doomed."

"That's what somebody hopes," Nora said.

The others looked at her attentively, but she did not go on. Tears slid down her cheeks and she wiped them with the towel she had been using to dry her hair. "I don't know ... I don't know ... I might have to go somewhere else. Driven out."

"Don't think about things like that," Mindy said. "It's too soon. Rest and get up your strength and we'll see what's to be done."

Kate felt powerless to say anything. First her husband, then her house. How could Nora bear it? What comfort could anybody offer? It was a cruel irony that the lightning had taken the Nobles' substantial year-round house, one of the older and best-built houses on the island, instead of one of the new pastel weekenders built for vacationers. She thought of all the old furniture the Nobles had brought with them—Phil's ancient roll-top desk, Nora's new, especially loved piano. Even if insurance enabled Nora to rebuild the house itself, some things were irreplaceable.

The men came in the back door, stamping rain and the black gunk of wet ashes from their feet. They hung up raincoats and walked into the kitchen, where Mindy met them with towels.

"With this rain there's no danger of the fire rekindling and spreading," Jim Preston said, reminding them all that he had the experience and authority of a former forest ranger. "I don't think there's a live coal left."

Retired five or six years, Jim still moved with a military bearing, kept his hair in a crew cut, and wore meticulously creased green duck trousers and shirts, which lacked the insignia but fit his lean and rangy frame as nattily as a forest-green uniform. His island car was an old Jeep with four-wheel drive and balloon tires and it was equipped with a tow chain, a shovel, and a pair of gigantic spotlights.

Kate always thought it was unfortunate that island property owners outlawed the practice of driving on the beach and the dunes about the time Jim had arrived so well equipped for rescuing the stuck. Still, he'd had enough occasions to rescue drivers who unwittingly veered off the shell roads into the deep sand and couldn't extricate themselves. Breakdowns of ancient cars were frequent enough to enlist his know-how and his emergency equipment. Kate wondered if he also carried a first-aid kit in his Jeep.

At that moment Dr. Wells, reaching for a towel, revealed a bandage on his hand. Emmy, ever motherly, particularly with this fortyish bachelor biologist, who was rather handsome when his bald head was covered, was instant sympathy.

"Vernon!" she cried. "You're hurt!"

"A little burn," he said bravely. "I picked up something at the fire I shouldn't have touched and seared my hand a little. Your husband took care of it. It's his burn ointment and his bandage."

Emmy gave Jim an approving smile.

"That's our Ranger Preston—ever ready," said young Dabney, mopping his dripping golden curls and grinning at Jim. When he was in college, he had spent a summer working with the state forest service and if he hadn't been rich, he probably would have stayed and been a solid and capable lieutenant to Jim Preston, Kate thought. Plenty of textile money and meeting and marrying Deb, heir to a real estate fortune, had committed him to a life of leisure.

But he had the nice manners of the well born, and he suddenly seemed to sense that in the midst of catastrophe banter was in bad taste.

"I'm sorry, Mrs. Noble," he said. "Deb and I would like to help any way we can. We've got to go back and pick up our boat at Key West and we've promised to take some friends on a cruise, so I don't think we'll be back on the island till spring. We'd be happy if you would use our house."

"Thank you, honey," Nora said. "I don't know. I'll see."

"Where is Deb?" Kate asked.

Young Dabney looked around uncertainly, as if he suddenly realized he had mislaid his little wife.

"Oh, I forgot!" he said. "She's still asleep."

The young, Kate thought indulgently, have the precious gift of drowning in sleep, oblivious to fire, flood, or calamity. She envied young Debbie.

Greg Herren stood at the edge of the group, mopping at his soaked running suit, his eyes on Nora. He looked tired. Smoke smeared his tanned cheeks and blackened the hollows under his eyes. He accepted a glass of brandy from Mindy and downed it at one gulp.

"I'll go on back to my place," he said. "Is anybody with a car going my way? I'd like to check my airplane as I go by."

"Sure," said Jim Preston. "Emmy and I will give you a ride."

"There's food left," Mindy said tentatively. "If anybody's hungry, we can make sandwiches."

Nobody was in the mood for food and they drifted out, a bedraggled little procession, stopping to hug or pat Nora, who smiled upon them tearfully.

The storm had vanished as rapidly as it appeared. No wind, no rain, no pyrotechnics. Kate noticed, as she climbed the back steps, that a whippoorwill had taken up his plaintive nightly cry in the woods back of her house. She checked the front of the house and stood spellbound at the beauty of the bay. The tide was out and the beach and sound waters, calm and still, seemed one—a lustrous shimmering sheet of silver that stretched into infinity.

Caught by the wonder of it, she pulled up a wet rocker and sat down. She had never seen the sound in this particular mood, so serene it was hard to believe that the weather which created it had brought the terrible, destructive storm such a short time ago. She felt an urge to get closer, and after a time she kicked off her shoes and walked down to the water's edge. Pepper normally would have dashed ahead of her, but, bruised and sore, he watched her go from his beach towel by the door, thumping his tail encouragingly.

A pale half-moon rode the western sky. Far out, too

far to identify and to determine if was moving or aground, Kate saw a sliver of black—the only boat visible on the silvery water.

Ash, she thought suddenly.

She had forgotten the old man's hazardous trip along the island and around the point in the middle of the storm.

She kept walking—and worrying.

He could have been swept overboard. His boat, leaky and unpredictable in calm weather, could have been swamped. She quickened her footsteps. If she cut through the dunes and the pine woods, she would make better time than if she followed the leisurely curve of the beach. Barefoot and mindful of snakes, she climbed a dune and slid to pine-straw-carpeted earth beyond it. There were trails through the woods, worn years ago by turpentine wagons, now all but obliterated by wind-blown sand, but she thought she had hit upon one and she trudged purposefully toward Ash's hut.

The moon, still pale, cast enough light for her to see the path, which curved inland. Suddenly it ended against a shell bank. Kate stopped, aghast. She had come upon the shell mound, the one most islanders avoided. They professed to be saving it for the study of anthropologists from the university, but Kate suspected the old superstitions circulated by Simolona people had had their effect. It was haunted.

She certainly wasn't afraid of ghosts, Kate told herself sturdily, but she didn't particularly fancy hanging around the shell mound after dark. It rose above her, luminous in the failing light, a strange and ancient structure for what purpose she wasn't sure. A graveyard? The university experts had said no. Just a haphazard sort of compost pile where the Indians had dumped their broken pots and piled their oyster shells? Maybe.

She searched the base for the continuation of the path. Palmettos crowded close and she saw no clear trail between the spiky green clumps. Suddenly out of the corner of her eye she saw movement on the mound. A raccoon, of course. The island was heavily populated with coons. Or maybe a feral cat. Or maybe her imagination.

She stood very still.

There was movement just beyond the crest of the mound. Of something bigger than a coon or a cat.

A person? Kate held her breath.

An oyster shell, dislodged by the movement above her, slid down the mound and fell at Kate's feet.

She turned and ran back toward the beach.

She was panting when she rounded the point and saw a cook fire in front of Ash's hut.

"Ash!" she called. "Ash?"

The old man answered and came out of his hut to meet her. He was breathless, too, she thought.

"Ash, I was worried about you. Afraid that storm got you!"

"Aw, you shouldn't a-worried," he protested. "I been through worse storms than that."

"What did you do?" Kate asked. "You couldn't ride that one out."

He shook his tangled gray head.

"Nope. I beached my skiff and walked in. Just got here."

"Was that you at the shell mound?" Kate asked, relieved.

"You see somebody there?" Ash asked.

"I couldn't see clearly," Kate admitted. "But somebody was there. They knocked loose an oyster shell and it fell at my feet. Spooky."

"Cats or one of them big coons," Ash said.

He paused. "Kate, best you stay away from that place. Some say it's devilishly ha'nted. I ain't seen, but I have heerd."

"Was that you I saw?" Kate persisted.

The old man busied around the fire. "I ain't skeered of ha'nts. But that place gives me the all-overs. I stay away."

Kate sighed. He wasn't going to answer her. As Mindy had said, Ash does what he wants to do.

She stood up. "I'll go. I'm glad you're safe. It was a bad storm. Lightning hit Nora's house and burned it to the ground."

"Oh, I seen the glow!" Ash said, astonished. "I didn't know! Lord God, what next?"

Kate stood silent, wanting to express sympathy to Ash but drained of feeling and words.

Ash recovered first. "I'll walk a piece with you," he said. "Best you go by the beach. Light tarries there."

For the first time Kate noticed that he was soaking wet. He might not have any dry clothes or he might have been too busy to change them.

"Never mind, Ash," she said. "I know my way. You get into some dry clothes and build up your fire. It's getting chilly." She smiled. "I'll bypass that old mound and its ha'nts."

The walk back to the cottage seemed longer than it did on a sunny day when she waded in the gentle combers, looking for shells, crabbing, or dragging her feet to send the stingrays scurrying. The sound was dark now. The lights of Simolona twinkled distantly. A buoy across the channel tolled its deep-throated bell, and in the far sky the lights on a television tower winked.

One of the lamps in her living room burned. It had been off when she went down to the beach, but then all the power was off. She was glad to see it—but had she left a lamp on? She couldn't remember. It had been a long, long day. She plodded slowly up the little boardwalk, reluctant to find out.

Pepper was silent except for the thumping of his tail. Then Nora spoke to her from a chair on the front porch.

"You've got company," she said.

"Oh, good," said Kate, dipping her feet in the plastic dishpan full of water all islanders had outside their doors to wash off sand before they could track it into the house. "I'm glad to see you. How did you get here?" She knew the Jeep had burned in the house fire.

"I walked," Nora said. "Did me good. Can I spend the night? I left a note for Mindy telling her I was going to."

"You know you can," Kate said, pulling up a chair close to Nora's. "Where was Mindy?"

"Asleep, I guess. Her bedroom door was closed and I didn't want to disturb her if she was taking a nap. I think she thought she had put me to bed for the night, but I couldn't sleep. Kate, somebody's trying to drive us from the island! Can you find out who and why?"

Kate sighed. In the past there had been efforts to tamper with life as they lived it on the island and those efforts had failed. The posh resort came to nothing. The movement to eliminate the ferry had been defeated. It no longer brought cars and it came but two days a week instead of daily, but it had not been eliminated. It was such a little island, less than a thousand acres, counting the bare shaft and the little wedge they called arrowhead. Who would want it? And for what purpose?

"I'll try, Nora," she said. "I gather you've decided to stay? This afternoon you said you didn't care what happened to the island."

"Well, I do care," Nora said. "It's still my home ... even—" She choked, "even if I don't have a home."

"Poor child," said Kate, leaning over to pat Nora on the shoulder. "You'll get another. You can share mine."

"Thank you," said Nora softly.

They were silent for a time, listening to the whisper of the waves and the intermittent call of the whippoorwill.

"Phil was the key to this push somebody has put on to get the island," Nora said after a moment. "He fought so hard to preserve it as a wildlife refuge and to limit building on it. You know we own a third of it, so that carried weight in Tallahassee."

Pepper came over and put his head on Kate's knee. The light from the living room showed up his cuts.

"What on earth?" cried Nora. "Pepper looks like he

was caught in a band saw. What happened to him?"

Kate explained. Nora listened and stroked Pepper's velvet muzzle, which he had moved to her knee.

"I don't know why Pepper and I would be the target for somebody who is trying to get the island," Kate said. "I don't own anything but this house and lot, and Pepper's only interest is chasing away intruders."

"That's it," said Nora. "Somebody came and Pepper got in his way. Are they knife wounds, or was it a whip?"

Kate said she didn't know, but if Nora was willing, they could use her boat and take Pepper to the vet the next day and transmit a story, which Kate would type into the little portable computer before she slept. She needed a real phone, not a marine radio, for that.

"Someday they will have telephones on the island," said Nora wanly, rising up to go to bed.

"Someday pigs will fly," Kate said flippantly, following her into the house.

She had fed Pepper and tucked Nora in bed with a cup of tea and was in the shower when she remembered young Sarah Langhorne. She wrapped a big beach towel around herself and knocked on Nora's door.

"You're not asleep?" she asked.

"Not yet," said Nora. "Want to talk?"

"No," said Kate. "I'm going to work, but I just thought of something. Sarah Langhorne didn't have anything to do with the island, did she? Why would she be a victim?"

"I don't know," said Nora tiredly. "You think. I can't."

Kate pulled out the little portable computer and wrote a story about Philip Noble's death and funeral and the terrible coincidence of his house burning down. She did not suggest that his death had been from any other than natural causes. There was time for that when she had more than an unsupported theory that sinister forces were at work on the island.

She went to sleep thinking of Sarah Langhorne, and determined to learn more about her on the morrow.

The next morning, as usual after a storm, the world sparkled. Prediction was for fair and colder weather, but the water promised to be calm and Kate and Nora, bundled up in jeans and padded nylon jackets, pulled knitted caps over their ears and set out for the mainland.

First they took Pepper to a vet, who examined the cuts on his head and didn't know what had caused them. A knife, maybe, or an old-fashioned rawhide whip. He wasn't sure. He put ointment on them, taped the deepest together, gave Pepper a shot, and dismissed him.

Kate phoned in her story from the pay station outside the grocery store and arranged to take a week of her vacation.

"If you're into murder, Katie, how about letting us know?" the city editor, Shell Shelnutt, said lightly.

"Murder?" Kate said innocently. "Whatever do you mean, sir?'

"If you haven't got a juicy homicide on your hands, you think life is not worth living," Shell grumbled. "Just let us know."

He hung up and Kate turned from the phone wondering if Shell could be prescient. Was it murder or not?

Nora had thought she had errands to do, but after

she got to Simolona she felt dull and uninterested in anything and told Kate she would sit in the car and wait for her to handle whatever it was she came for.

"I want to talk to Sarah Langhorne's parents," Kate told her. "And maybe some of the people at Florida State."

"How do you know where to find the Langhornes?"

"Emmy mentioned that they live in Waycross, Georgia."

"Are you going all the way over there?"

"Not if I can get them on the phone," Kate said, and went back into the phone booth to make her call.

The Langhornes were at home and they were willing, even eager, to talk about their daughter.

Kate came to the point. Did they believe Sarah had committed suicide?

"That's what the sheriff thought," said the father on one extension. "We had to accept that."

"I don't accept it at all!" declared Mrs. Langhorne from another extension. "Sarah was very happy. She was doing well at school and she had a beau. I think that she was very much in love."

"Did you know the beau?" asked Kate, pleased with the old-fashioned synonym for what was probably a lover.

"No," Mrs. Langhorne said hesitantly. "I don't think she mentioned his name. But I asked her to bring him to visit and she said she would sometime soon."

"Was he somebody she knew at the university?"

Mrs. Langhorne was silent and Mr. Langhorne spoke up. "No! I think he was somebody on that island. Else why would she want to spend so much time on that god-forsaken place?"

"She liked the water and she was ... a nature lover," the mother said defensively. "Since she was a little girl she's been crazy about birds and—"

"I think it was a man, Mrs. Mulcay," the father said. "And I don't think he was much good because he did not come forward when we had to give her up for dead."

"Could she have simply gone somewhere?" Kate asked.

"Disappear and leave us worrying? Never!" cried Mrs. Langhorne. "Sarah wasn't that kind of girl. She was a home person. She stayed in touch with us. Why, we talked on the phone at least once a week."

Kate could hear Mr. Langhorne clearing his throat. "Mrs. Mulcay, where are you calling from? Could you give me that number?"

Puzzled, Kate gave him the number.

"I'll call you back," he said.

Could he have been trying to get rid of her, or did he have something more to say? Uncertain, Kate stood by the telephone booth, fending off two teenagers who had come up with coins in their hands ready to make a call.

"I'm expecting a very important call," she told them. "If you don't mind ... I think it might take only a minute or two."

"Sure," said the boy. "There's another phone over at the filling station. We'll go over there."

They were halfway across the parking lot when the phone rang. Mr. Langhorne.

"I had to wait till Lou left," he said. "She was on her

way out the door to some kind of meeting with a friend and I knew they'd be gone in a minute. She doesn't know this, Mrs. Mulcay, and I don't want to tell her. They found Sarah's sweater and pieces of her blue jeans in the water. Them goddamn sharks got my daughter!"

His voice was rough with tears. Kate made sounds of sympathy and didn't ask the question foremost in her mind. Why would the girl he described be swimming in the cold water of the cut in December?

Back at her car, Kate found Nora hunched down in her jacket, her head barely visible over the top of the seat. For a second, alarm swept over Kate. Had something happened to Nora?

She rushed to open the door and Nora stirred sleepily and smiled up at her guiltily.

"I sort of dozed off," she said.

"That's good," Kate told her. "You're all tired out. A nap will do you good."

"So much I meant to do," mumbled Nora. "Now I don't much care."

"I know," said Kate, reaching for the ignition key. "Let me handle some of the stuff for you. Didn't you plan to report the fire to your insurance company? Give me the names and numbers, if you remember them, and I'll call for you."

Nora remembered the Tallahassee agent's name but no numbers. Kate could get that from information. She wrote down the name and turned to Nora.

"Look, what do you think about calling the fire marshal to investigate the fire? The county does have one, doesn't it?"

"I don't know," said Nora. "Phil ..."

They both sighed and looked out on the tidy little street, which was very quiet in the morning light.

Kate pulled herself together. "Suppose I ask your lawyer—Cecil James, isn't it?—to get an investigation going? He probably knows the fire marshal or can get his name."

With that settled, she took another tack.

"You told me that two other people on the island died recently. What about them?"

Nora rallied slightly, sat up straight in her seat, and pushed up her cap. She took a deep breath.

"Finley Sawyer—I know you must remember him. He first came to the island with some ornithological group checking the bird population. He was a big environmentalist. He bought the Upsons' house down the beach. He and his wife and their little girls had just moved in when they all got violently sick.

"He kept trying to trace it down and finally made Berma and the children stay in town until he found out what was causing it. He'd get nauseated and so limp and lethargic he couldn't seem to do a thing. He loved the place, too. It was last fall and he came a lot by himself, trying to get the house painted and winterized. The children were in school and Berma stayed with them. So that was all right. He liked to light a fire in that big rock fireplace and sleep on the rug in front of it when the nights got cold."

"And he was poisoned?" Kate asked.

"Phil and I thought so," Nora said. "I think his doctor said it was something else. Maybe some kind of ferocious allergy. I don't remember what."

"Do you know how to get in touch with Berma?"

Nora shook her head. "She was from New Orleans or some other place in Louisiana. I don't remember. She put the house on the market and went home to her family. I can't tell you their names."

"Who bought the house?"

"I don't know," Nora said. "I don't believe it's sold yet. In fact, I'm sure it's standing there empty."

"The other person?" Kate prodded. "You said a man in a boat."

"Oh, you knew Paul Lewis," Nora said. "A lawyer from some little town up in Alabama. He was retired, but he talked law all the time."

Nora grinned. "Phil liked him, but I found him kind of tiresome. I think his wife must have, too, because she never came with him. He showed us pictures of their home—a big antebellum mansion they inherited—and he said his wife didn't want to leave it. But he loved to fish and sail and he came a lot by himself or with some man friend."

"He was by himself when he was found dead in his boat?"

"He was staying in his house on the island by himself, but that morning he and Phil had been together. He wanted to rehash all those old fights we had to keep the ferry coming to the island and show his knowledge of the law. He went with Phil to the county commissioners' meeting and Phil said he got mad when they said the state could no longer afford ferry service to this island.

He made a speech and threatened to sue. It was his theory that the state had to provide access to a citizen's home, and in the case of an island, a ferry is tantamount to a road."

"What happened?"

"Nothing. The county people said it was a state matter and some jerk in the back of the room hollered out that it wasn't up to local taxpayers to support a ferry to get rich people to their vacation homes." She snorted. "Rich people! How many of us are rich?"

Kate shrugged. "Not present company, certainly. Then was he found dead?"

"The next morning. Ray Ellis saw him when he went down to the ferry dock. His boat was tied up under that boat shed where it was sort of dark and I guess nobody had been close enough to see him before. He was stretched out with his hands crossed on his chest."

"And the cause of death?" Kate persisted.

"You know—the usual—heart failure. Brought on, they decided, by acute alcoholism. Only he didn't drink."

The two women sat quite still for several minutes, staring out at the quiet street with its little palm trees glistening from last night's stormy rain.

"It's funny," mused Nora, "that Phil and the others—except Sarah, I guess—loved the island and really worked to preserve it. All three of them worked hard to get it declared a wildlife refuge." She bit her lips and ducked her head. "I think they were killed for it."

Kate sighed and started the car. "We'll see what we will see."

"You know how Phil loved Shakespeare," Nora said

after a moment. "I keep thinking that like Julius Caesar he was killed by somebody he loved and trusted, some Brutus."

. "Maybe," said Kate noncommittally, but her mind went back to passages memorized in sophomore English: "Ingratitude more strong than traitors' arms quite vanquished him, then burst his mighty heart." With Caesar the actual method had been knives. With Phil ... was it snakes?

Young Bert was again dockside when Kate and Nora headed for the Nobles' boat. This time he had no fishing pole but twisted his young hands with their big knuckles nervously and swallowed hard as he attempted to speak.

"Can I hep you load?" he finally asked.

"Aw, Bert," said Nora affectionately, "that's very good of you, but we haven't been shopping this time. Catch us on grocery day."

"I heard about the fire, Mrs. Noble," he said. "Mama said if you need a place to stay here on the main, you'd be welcome at our house. It ain't much, but ..."

"It's a good house," said Nora warmly, "and you and your mother are wonderful to offer it. I certainly will take you up on it if I need to stay in Simolona. Right now I'm staying with my friend, Mrs. Mulcay."

Bert bobbed his red head. "Yes'm, I know."

Nora took the left-hand seat in the boat and left the lines to Kate, who pulled the loop off the bollard and paused, looking at Bert. He obviously had something on his mind. She waited.

Finally he blurted, "I got a extry can of gas! Thought you might need it."

"Thank you, Bert," Kate said. "I forgot about gas. We could run out. As you know, islanders always need gas."

He motioned her toward an old truck across the street and Kate returned the bowline to the post and followed him.

"I didn't want Mrs. Noble to hear," the boy said hastily as he reached for a five-gallon red plastic gas can. "But Sarah Langhorne was pregnant. Don't seem like she would commit suicide."

"How did you happen to know that?" Kate asked. Sarah was older, came from another town, and was a university student. It didn't seem likely that she would have any association with this kid.

"She told me," he said. "She come over here in the Prestons' boat a lot and one day it wouldn't start. I got it going for her. She got sick and started puking. I told her it must be the smell of gasoline and she said no, it was a baby. She was planning on getting married."

"Did she tell you the name of her fiancé?"

"Her what?" Bert asked, and then rallied. "Oh, you mean her boyfriend. No'm, she didn't."

"Do you think it was somebody at the university?"

Bert hesitated. "I think it was somebody around here. She said they was going to have a island wedding and she would invite me."

He paused. "She was a real friendly girl."

Must have been, Kate thought sourly as she picked up the gift of gas and turned toward the boat.

All the way across the sound she mused on the matter of young Sarah and her planned island wedding. It certainly didn't seem to have any connection with Phil

Noble's death or the deaths of those other two men. It was probably Nora's fancy that they were all tied together. But it was odd, as Mr. Langhorne suggested, that the prospective groom did not come forward when the girl disappeared and that his name was still unknown. Why the secrecy?

Mindy was on the dock when they reached the island, her silver chignon covered with a knitted cap, which matched the tweed mohair sweater she wore, which matched the tweed mohair tailored slacks.

"Oh, my poor babies," she said, "stirring around in this cold wind! Come on up to the house. I have a fire going and a pot of gumbo on the stove."

"I believe I will," Nora said. "You, too, Kate?"

Kate shook her head. "Thank you, Mindy. I'm going to take Pepper home and tend to a few things."

She didn't know what those things were—and she did know. Sarah Langhorne disappeared from Ash's end of the island. She needed to see Ash.

7

►**B**efore Kate started her car, she sat quietly looking at the white sand and the waters of the gulf, today as smooth as glass. She had no reason to worry about young Sarah, but since Nora had mentioned Shakespeare and Mindy had mentioned their stirring around, she thought of poor old Macbeth, a warrior but a wimp, hoping to homicidally clear the way to be king "without stir." She knew from experience that she couldn't solve anything without stir.

On impulse she decided to stop by the little graveyard and take another look at the stone marker her parents had erected for Sarah.

Beyond the gate and the marker she saw movement. When she got closer, she saw it was Ash, facedown beside Philip Noble's grave.

"No!" she cried and started running. Ash could not be dead!

"Ash!" she cried. And he lifted his head.

"Hidy-do, Kate," the old man said, looking up and smiling cordially. "How you?"

"Ah, Ash, I thought you were dead," said Kate, slumping down on the sand on the other side of the grave.

"Not yit," said Ash, "but purty nigh."

Then Kate saw that he had a plastic bucket of seashells beside him and a couple of little channeled whelk shells in his hand.

"What are you doing?"

"Got to thinking them shells I put on Philip's grave yestiddy wasn't purty enough. I found these and decided to lick my calf over."

Kate studied the long white mound that covered Phil and sighed. Ash had made it pretty with seashells, but it was small comfort for the loss of a friend.

"You thought a lot of him, didn't you?" she asked at last.

"Phil was my pa and my preacher and the guardeen of my soul," Ash said, sitting up and looking out to sea. "I told him just about evvathing."

"Did you tell him about Sarah Langhorne?" Kate asked daringly.

"I did," Ash said soberly. "He said I done right and to say no more about it. Least said, quickest mended, he said."

"What did you do, Ash?"

"I gathered up that young'un's bones that washed ashore and give them a decent burial."

"Ah, Ash, that was good of you. Where did you bury them?"

The old man looked around and lowered his voice to a whisper.

"In the shell mound, where they wouldn't be disturbed."

They sat quietly for a time, listening to the north wind soughing in the pines and palmettos and causing the sand to drift in little whirls around the graves.

"Why, Ash? Why did Phil want you to keep it a secret? Why not tell her parents?"

"They was already so bad off with grief, Phil said."

Kate nodded. "I suppose he was wise. But why did she go out into the cut? Did you see her?"

"To my shame I did," Ash said. He carefully placed a whelk on the grave and turned to face Kate. "I told you I ain't always done good, like Nora said about me. I set there in my house a-looking out the door and I seen that girl a-setting on the sand kindly waiting. A boat come up in the channel and she stood up and waved, but it didn't come any closer. So afore I could of stopped her she waded out and begun to swim."

"And then?"

"A shark hit her and she went under."

"And the boat? Who was in it? Did they try to get to her?"

Ash shook his head.

"Revved up the engine and took off."

"Oh, Ash, how horrible!" cried Kate. "To leave that girl to such an awful death!"

"She didn't scream but onct, and that was cut off. I took my skiff and went out there, but there was nothing left until the bones was et clean and washed ashore with some of her clothes."

Kate felt rising nausea. *I'm going to be sick,* she thought. *It's the most hideous death I can think of. Why would anybody entice a girl to swim in waters everybody on the island knew were dangerous?*

"Did you see who was in the boat, Ash?"

The old man shook his head. "The sun was agin me. I couldn't tell."

"Well, whose boat was it?"

"Philip asked them same questions and I'll tell you what I told him. Hit was a new boat to me. I keep looking, but I ain't seen hit since."

"Too big to come into the shallow water?"

"I'd a brought it in, Kate, to save that girl. Even if hit meant running aground and setting there till next week."

"I know you would, Ash. I think anybody decent would have." She stood up. "If you saw that boat again, would you recognize it?"

Ash nodded. "Hit jes' ain't a sound boat. Me and Phil went a-looking and I ain't seen hit again. Not blue and white like most island boats, but black. Death black."

Kate shivered.

There were black boats along the coast, but not many. Even the shrimpers and mullet fishermen only used black for trim. It might be a waste of time, but she was going to find that boat.

She turned to Ash. "Thank you for telling me. I'll hold it in confidence."

"Best you do," the old man said. "Phil said even the knowing of hit is dangerous."

Kate hurried back to Mindy's to ask permission to borrow Nora's boat.

"Some things I forgot about," she explained hastily.

"You mean at the newspaper?" Nora asked, looking up from the sofa where she rested under a bright plaid blanket.

"Hmn. Need to make some calls," Kate said.

"Go ahead, take the boat," Nora said. "I think there's plenty of gas, but you have Bert's contribution if you need it." She smiled wanly.

"You need anything, Mindy?" Kate called with the de rigeur shoregoing courtesy of islanders.

"Yes," said Mindy, emerging from her bedroom. "Bread, of course. All I have is a regular Ila loaf." They smiled together. The regular Ila loaf was a dampish misshapen loaf that got hit by spray and mangled in crossing. "And a bottle of brandy," added Mindy. "Here's the money."

Kate waved the money aside. "I'll keep track and bill you when I get back."

On shore she went first to the marina to look at boats. Bemis, the young man who ran the marina, was on the telephone in his little office overlooking the harbor and he waved at her and went on talking.

"Just looking, Bemis," Kate said, and went out into the yard.

All the boats, tip-tilted on trailers, were new stock Bemis was offering for sale, all glistening white. Kate turned to the long shed with its tiers of boats Bemis stored there, a few of them for Ila Islanders, most of them for people who had cottages on the bigger barrier islands down the coast and came only during vacations and school holidays.

Kate walked down the row checking hulls. All white or white and blue. The rumble of a tractor sounded behind her and she turned to see a new lavender-blue bass boat, iridescent and as shiny as a Christmas tree ornament, coming her way on a forklift. She hurried to get out of the way, squeezing into a spot between two powerboats.

"Hi, Miss Kate!" called Bert from the driver's seat, cutting the engine. "I didn't know you were here. Good thing you got out of the way."

"Yeah," said Kate wryly. "I'd hate to be run down by a boat on dry land."

Bert climbed off the seat and walked to meet her.

"You wasn't thinking of buying another boat, was you?"

"Just looking, Bert," Kate said again.

"Plenty of bargains this time of year," Bert offered.

Kate shook her head. "I was thinking rental, Bert. Does Bemis ever rent his boats?"

"Not that I know of," the boy said. "You have to go to Apalach for that. They get a lot of tourists. Couple run a tourist court on the river have a few boats they rent."

"You know the name so I can look them up in the phone book?"

Bert wasn't sure how the place was listed, but he knew where it was. He started to tell Kate where to turn on the river road and then he stopped.

"I can go with you and show you, Miss Kate. If you can wait till I put this bass boat on the shelf."

"I'll wait," Kate said, glad of his company.

The river road was beautiful, with giant oak trees draped with curtains of gray Spanish moss meeting overhead and tall ferns, now winter-browned, along the shoulder. The fishing camp–motel was in a grove of wind-twisted oaks overlooking the river. Bert directed Kate to the office at the head of a long dock, where a dozen boats were tied up.

She knocked and waited while Bert walked out to the end of the pier.

Her knock on the door echoed with an unmistakable nobody-home sound and Kate was about to give up and join Bert on the wharf when he came back grinning.

"Funny name on that old Boston whaler down there. Did you ever see a boat named *Hell'n'back?*"

"Never," said Kate, smiling. She followed Bert back along the little quay. He pointed.

The *Hell'n'back* was a black boat! A deep-hulled black boat.

Kate stood looking at it, not savoring the racy name as Bert was, but wondering if it was the "death black" boat Ash had seen.

They heard a pickup truck arriving in the oak grove behind them. A fat man in a bright blue polyester jumpsuit and a red billed cap with BUD on the front got out and came toward them, causing the dock to quiver convulsively under his weight.

"You all looking for a boat?" he asked. Then he recognized Bert. "Hi, Red! You going fishing?"

"No, sir, Mr. Mann," Bert said. "Just come with this lady—Miss Kate—to look."

Mr. Mann took off his cap and bobbed his head at Kate. "What can I do for you, ma'am?"

"I was thinking about renting a boat," Kate lied. "You do rent them, don't you?"

"Lige does," said the man. "He owns this joint, but him and his wife have gone off yonder somewhere to visit her folks and I'm just looking after the motel till they get back. He's got two boats that he lets regular customers have. You want to see them?"

"Is that Boston whaler one of them?" Kate asked.

"Aw, no," said Mr. Mann. "That's Lige's personal boat. He will take you deep-sea fishing in it. But he's particular who drives it."

"It's in good shape?" Kate asked.

"Sure is," said Mr. Mann. "Lige keeps it up to snuff. Now, over here ..." He led the way to a couple of aging launches tied to iron pins driven into the bank on the opposite side of the quay. Mud squished around Kate's sneakers, but she looked obediently at all the charms of the for-rent craft and told Mr. Mann she would think about it.

They were back at the car when she turned to Mr. Mann and said, "You don't happen to know if Lige rented the Boston whaler to somebody last December?"

The fat man let out a bellow of laughter.

"Rent? I reckon not! Somebody stole that boat! How did you hear about it?"

Kate was hard-pressed for an explanation, but Bert saved her.

"We heard at the marina that Lige was looking for

his boat," he put in. "Didn't he find it somewhere odd?"

"Odd is right," said Mann. "Up the river, tied to the dock in front of some Yankee's house. Folks were up in Ohio or some place like that and there was the *Hell'n'back* tied to their dock. Surprise, surprise!" He chortled again. "Lige never found out how it got there."

Then that's the boat, Kate said to herself. *Now to find out who borrowed it.*

Kate got bread and brandy for Mindy and let Bert out at the marina. Ray Ellis, the ferryboat captain, was putting gas in his personal boat. He turned and waved when he saw Kate.

"Need a ride?" he asked, returning the gas nozzle to the pump and walking toward the car. "I'm going that way."

"Thank you," Kate said, "but I have Nora's boat. You going fishing?"

He shook his golden head. "Just thought I'd pay my respects to Nora. Where is she staying since the fire?"

"She's at Mindy's now," Kate said. "I'll probably take her home with me when I get over there." She wanted to ask Raynor about the black boat, but some impulse or instinct caused her to hold back. Instead she asked, "You ever go deep-sea fishing? I have some friends in Atlanta who are crazy to get out in the gulf and catch barricudas. And maybe sharks. Do you know where they can get a boat to take them out?"

"I wouldn't take this one too far out, especially in winter weather." He nodded toward his boat, which bobbed in the brown river water. "One of the big excursion boats over in Carrabelle takes out fishing parties. You could ask there."

"I think they had in mind renting something and making a day-long cruise of it," Kate said.

She looked up and Ellis was staring at her wordlessly, his usually charming smile absent, his sea-green eyes frosty. He turned away, and Kate shrugged and started her car.

Back at Mindy's house she found a gathering of island friends sitting around the living room fire.

Kate delivered the bread and brandy, declined Mindy's money, and went to warm herself at the fireplace.

"Kate," Nora said softly from her seat on the sofa. "Jim and Emmy are thinking about selling their house."

"No!" said Kate, disbelieving. "Why?"

"I guess we don't love the island the way we used to," said Emmy. "Too many awful things have happened. Even Vernon is thinking about giving up and going elsewhere."

Kate turned to face the biologist. "But I thought you found the island home for a rare lot of animals and birds and marine life."

"I did," Dr. Wells said soberly. "There's no finer place for my work—and my enjoyment. But it's changing, Kate, changing. I don't know. I haven't decided yet."

Kate looked around the circle of faces, rosy in the firelight. "Have you had any offers from prospective buyers?"

Emmy looked uncomfortable. "We've been talking ...

well, a friend of ours, a real estate agent, mentioned it to us. She has a client, she said. I wasn't interested then, but since Phil ... Well, it's not going to be the place we love."

"What about you, Mindy?" Kate asked as Mindy came in from the kitchen carrying a tray of sandwiches and coffee. Mindy stood a minute looking from face to face. The oldest and the handsomest person in the room with her white hair and black eyes and black eyebrows, she dominated the gathering.

"I don't know," she said at last. "I don't know. But what would the island be to me without you all, my dear, dear friends?"

"Kate?" Nora asked. "Would you sell?"

"I haven't even thought about it. How about you?"

Nora gazed steadily into the fire. "Phil wouldn't want me to."

"Even for money?" asked Raynor Ellis, who had come into the kitchen and was quietly divesting himself of windproof jacket and cap.

"Especially not for money," said Nora, smiling ruefully. "Phil thought our house and two lots were a gracious plenty for our use. He wanted the rest of the land we own to be a wildlife refuge. That's why he would never let it be divided into lots and sold."

"Opposed to any more building, was he?" asked Greg Herren, seated next to Nora on the sofa.

Nora turned to face him. "Not all building. He opposed anything commercial and, of course, condos and apartment complexes. He loved the island people and he thought an occasional new house on the island was exciting. But he didn't want to see it overbuilt or crowded. You know, Mindy ... you and Kate know how Phil felt."

"If you don't mind my asking," put in Greg, "how much of the island do you own?"

"One-third," said Nora. "Dr. Wooten at the university and a cousin of Phil's, Dr. Durant, who is also a professor, have the other two-thirds."

"You own about three or four hundred acres, I guess," Mindy ventured.

"I guess," Nora said tiredly. "I don't have the papers here now." She choked and looked out the window, where the wind blew all that remained of her house—ashes and charred fragments of wood—over the sand. Even indoors they could smell the stench of wet ashes.

"Never mind, honey," Kate said gently. "We can get duplicates of everything at the courthouse when and if you need them."

"And you probably have a safe-deposit box at the bank," put in Greg.

Nora looked uncertain.

"It's not important now," Kate said with decision. "We can look into all that later. Come on, Nora, and let's get to my house and dog before it gets dark and colder."

"Oh, poor Pepper," said Nora. "I forgot about him. Did you all see what happened to Kate's Pepper-dog?"

"I did," said Mindy, "and it was grisly. Nice dog like that being whipped or knifed."

The others registered varying degrees of shock and Kate stood up and pulled Nora to her feet.

"We're going, too," Jim Preston said. "We walked

down the beach and I always feel better cutting through the woods trail before it gets too dark."

"I'll walk with you as far as my house," Dr. Wells said.

Kate followed Emmy into the bedroom, where Mindy had put their jackets.

"Em," she said softly, "did you know who Sarah Langhorne was seeing over here?"

Emmy turned from the jacket-laden bed in surprise.

"Why, no," she said. "Nobody while she was at my house. She and Emaline went out with boys at the university but nobody down here. Kate, you may not have noticed, but there aren't any young men their age around here anymore. Used to be, but they have grown up and gone away. Who said Sarah had a romance going here?"

"I talked to her parents," Kate said. "The father seemed to think she was involved with some man on the island and that was the reason she spent so much time here."

"Well, I like that!" cried Emmy. "As if our hospitality wasn't attraction enough!"

"Oh, Em." Kate sighed. "She was a young girl. Hospitality is fine and I'm sure yours is top-flight, but love is even better. How often was she here?"

Emmy stood holding her jacket and trying to think. "A lot," she said after awhile. "She came almost every time Emaline came and, as you know, the last time she was here she stayed in the house by herself. I'm sure her parents fault us for that."

"I don't think so," said Kate. "At least they didn't

mention it. Was she always with Emaline when they came, or did they go their separate ways?"

"Oh, Kate, I don't know!" Emmy said impatiently. "You know all of us on the island have always made a practice of turning our children loose here and letting them do what they want to do. They walked and swam together and crabbed and picked berries and lay around the house swinging in the hammock and reading. Emaline went fishing with her father some, but Sarah always begged off that. A few times she was late getting here. Emaline always comes on Friday after her last class and sometimes Sarah would wait and come on the Saturday afternoon ferry."

Mindy came in before Kate could ask another question, which, if she had spoken her thoughts, would have been, did they come down from Tallahassee together and did Sarah stop off and spend the night in a motel?

She was glad in a way that she didn't have the opportunity of pursuing that line. She could almost hear Emmy's screech of dismay. Emmy was not only highly moral but monumentally shockable.

Mindy's sandwiches had taken the edge off their appetites, and Nora opted for an early bedtime sans supper. Kate took Pepper for a run on the beach, which he turned into a sedate stroll at her heels, and brought him back and fed him.

She fished out a notebook and a black newspaper copy pen and sat down before the fire to try to make some sense of the macabre events on the island. She put first—not because it was of primary importance but because it was uppermost in her mind—the question:

The man? That meant to Kate—and she hoped to nobody else who might accidentally see the note—the man Sarah was seeing, the man who got her pregnant, the man in the black boat who enticed her to her death.

Beneath that she wrote: *Profit*. Who would profit by disposing of a leading islander like Phil and frightening the others away? She added the names of Finley Sawyer and Paul Lewis without much hope. Their deaths might have been from natural causes, Sawyer's from some virulent allergy, and perhaps Paul Lewis was a closet drunkard and more subject to acute alcoholism than Nora knew.

Kate sat a long time looking at her list. She wished for Benjy, whose years as a homicide detective might have helped him to make some sense out of the whole complicated muddle. He would have added, she knew, a question about the feral cat in her house, the open window in the utility room, the injuries to Pepper. He would have wanted to know something she had forgotten: How did a dog who lived where there was only white sand, pine needles, and salt water get mud on his feet and legs?

Kate tried to think where the nearest mudhole was located. There was a brackish pond a mile to the east—black as night, even brooding and somber in the daytime. Kate always hurried past it on her daytime walks. Cottonmouth moccasins proliferate in such places, and—Kate swallowed hard at the thought—alligators! More than one islander had seen them. Had somebody tried to feed Pepper to alligators?

Kate stood up so fast she dropped her notebook and

stepped on Pepper's tail, which curved around the bottom of her chair. At that moment there was a knock at the back door, followed by the islanders' customary "Hello! Anybody home?"

Pepper went into a frenzy of barking, rushing ahead of Kate to the door. She grasped his collar in one hand and opened the door with the other. Greg Herren stood there.

"Hush, Pepper. A friend," she said, hoping it was so.

Pepper subsided but stood beside her, alert to appraise the visitor.

"Come in, Greg," Kate said, and Greg, one eye on the dog, stepped inside.

He looked around the room. "I thought Nora might be up. Has she gone to bed already?"

"She was pretty tired," Kate said. "But won't you sit down anyhow? I'll poke up the fire. It's getting nippy out there."

The big man shed his baseball cap and down vest and put them on a chair by the door. He took a wicker rocker by the fire, holding out his hands to the blaze.

"Can I get you a drink?" Kate asked.

He shook his head. "Mindy plied us with enough of that brandy you brought to get us soused. Took the walk down here to sober me up."

Kate laughed. "Mindy's hospitality is legendary. I reckon she can't get over the rich woman's feeling that she has to provide food and drink for everybody, especially us island peasants."

"Tell me about Mindy," Greg said. "Formerly rich only? Rich no more?"

"Oh, Mindy's perfectly outspoken about her poverty," Kate said lightly. "I'm sure she'd tell you that she lives in what she stylishly calls 'reduced circumstances.' That's better than being what the rest of us would call flat-out broke, isn't it?"

Greg laughed aloud, a pleasant sound, Kate decided.

"I've tried it both ways," he said, "and Mindy's way is better. I worked for a newspaper in my youth, supporting a wife and baby on twenty-five dollars a week. We knew that wasn't 'reduced circumstances.' It was flat-out, uncompromising, beat-down penury."

Kate grinned. "Yep, I remember such paydays. But I didn't know that you have a family. Nobody mentioned a wife when they told me you are a new-hatched Ila Islander. Does she come down here with you?"

He shook his head. "Poverty finally did us in. She left me and took our little boy. He's grown now and I see him on college holidays sometimes. She married again. I didn't. The irony, of course, is that I left newspapering, dabbled in politics, got a job with the government, and now can afford the rent and the grocery bill."

"And a nice airplane and holidays in Florida," Kate interjected.

He smiled. "Until it's time for the thousand-hour check. Then I wonder if I can afford that airplane or these island visits."

They sat on in a comfortable silence, unbroken except by the turning of an oak chunk in the fireplace. Kate involuntarily yawned and Greg promptly stood up.

"I had no reason to impose my company on you this late," he said. "I just feel rotten about what has happened to Phil and Nora and I keep thinking that there should be something I could do. I know Nora thinks it's murder and probably arson, too. And she has asked you to investigate. If I can help ..." he smiled down at her and reached for his vest and cap, "call on me. I covered police a little while when I worked for a newspaper."

"Did you?" said Kate breathlessly. "Well, my husband—"

"I know," Greg said, turning from the door. "A rather celebrated criminal investigator. I've heard of Major Benjamin Mulcay.

Well! Kate said to herself when she had closed the door behind him, *And I thought he was a jerk! An old police reporter and he's heard of Benjy.*

The combination of attributes cheered Kate, so she looked in on Nora to tell her, just in case she happened to be awake. But Nora was sleeping soundly and the only thing Kate could think to do to celebrate this pleasant turn was to pour herself a small glass of sherry to have at the ready on her bedside table when she had had a shower and washed her hair.

8

➤ Kate was up before Nora with the coffeepot going. She considered a day on the island wasted if she missed the sunrise, and this one was going to be spectacular—a blazing ball of fire set precisely on the barb of arrowhead, where it was thrust out into the still misty waters of the gulf.

A bank of clouds, foretelling rain, seemed to be ignited by the sun's flame. *Sailor, take warning,* Kate quoted contentedly, feeling temporarily lulled by red sky at morning. If it stormed, she would not feel compelled to leave the house. She could make a pot of soup, fill the woodbox, and read some of the books she had stacked up waiting for her.

Pepper rattled the dried food in his dish and scratched at the screen door to get out.

"Feeling better, old scout?" Kate asked, patting his taped head. He wagged his tail and trotted down the steps to demonstrate a return to vigor.

Kate heard water running in the bathroom and went

to set out a cup and cream and sugar for Nora. She would get around to breakfast later.

Nora came out wearing one of Benjy's old beach robes, a lurid Roman striped terry-cloth toga. Kate realized that her friend had nothing left of her own. She should suspend all other activity for the day and take Nora to town to buy something to wear.

Nora, who also liked the sunrise, took her cup to the back steps and, wrapping the voluminous robe around her, sat down. Her face, almost café au lait from outdoors on the sunny island, looked pale and thin under the neutral cap of gray hair. Her eye sockets were dark and her cheeks seemed hollowed out.

She drank her coffee silently, her eyes on the sunrise.

All that she loved is gone, Kate thought pityingly. *"For this she scooped her temples thin,"* she mentally quoted lines from her favorite poet, Elinor Wylie. *"For this she starred her eyes with salt ... she deserved a better fate than this."*

Nora deserved a better fate and Kate didn't know how Nora would ever find it for herself. Lacking anything else to say, she forced a cheery tone.

"Want to go shopping today? You are the only woman I ever knew who literally hasn't got a thing to wear."

Nora smiled faintly.

"Except for sanitation, I couldn't care. But you have to have something to wear while you wash what you have on. I was going to put my sweater and shirt and jeans in your washing machine when I get up my strength."

"Sure," said Kate. "You can do that while I cook us some breakfast. If you make a list, we can hit the stores fast."

"Mindy mentioned that," Nora said. "You know she is different from you and me. She really likes to shop. She suggested that we could make it a quick trip if Greg Herren would check out Phil's airplane for us. I can't fly it, but Mindy can, you know."

"That's a good idea," Kate said. "If Mindy will fly you over, I might stay here and poke around a bit."

"That way we can leave you the boat," Nora said.

Mindy had already arranged with Greg to check out Phil's little plane and he was there when Kate drove to the landing strip with Nora wearing clean, slightly dampish jeans and one of Kate's sweaters because her own needed more time in the dryer. Mindy had climbed into the cockpit and was warming up the engine and checking the controls. Greg boosted Nora into the passenger seat and removed the wheel chocks. They watched the small bird taxi down the parking area to the landing strip and turn into the wind for the takeoff.

"Phil loved that little plane," Kate said.

"I think it was love of that little plane that killed him," Herren said soberly.

Kate turned to search his face.

"Look," he said, "I didn't have time to bury this before Nora got here. But look what I found coiled on the dash when I started to get in the airplane."

He led the way to the weeds at the edge of the field and pointed to a four-foot rattlesnake.

"Oh, my God!" gasped Kate, backing away.

"He's dead," Herren said. "I think he was dead when somebody put him there. But Phil didn't know that. He just came out to look over his plane, as he did every morning. Even if he didn't fly it much, he kept it in shape, wiping it off and checking the gas and sometimes moving it to another tie-down to rotate the tires. Everybody knew that."

"And everybody knew how he felt about snakes," Kate said faintly.

"Yeah, they did," Greg said.

The sun was well up in the sky when Kate got back to her car. It had burned off the color that had promised a squally day and the gulf seemed blue and benign. Kate felt an unaccountable urge to see all of the island, which suddenly seemed threatened.

She had never taken a boat through the cut between islands and around to the end of Ila's barbed point they called the arrowhead by herself. She and Benjy went together and fishing boats from Simolona often anchored there in the shelter of the tall dunes, which made wings to the wedge-shaped head of the island. She wasn't secure enough in her seamanship to feel safe in a small boat that far from habitation if a storm came up. But the Nobles' boat was a little bigger, and the gulf was calm today.

She went back to her cottage to put Pepper indoors and grab up a poncho and tuck an apple and a sandwich in its pocket. As an afterthought she got Benjy's deep-sea fishing rod and tackle box. She didn't really intend to fish, but it was an excuse for the excursion if anybody wanted to know.

The Nobles' boat started promptly after Kate had checked and refilled the gas tank from Bert's can. She hurried to run it out to the mouth of the harbor out of hearing of the loiterers on the dock in case some of them would assume she was going ashore and ask for a ride or give her a list of errands. As an afterthought she checked the life jackets under the dash and found half a dozen, all in good order. Typical of the Nobles, she thought sadly.

The run around the island produced the old surge of pleasure which rose up in her when she and Benjy first came that way and picked the spot for their little house. All the houses seemed to be drowsing in the morning light. Not even a tendril of smoke rose from a chimney. The barge which had slumbered in the channel had moved on. Shrimpers had headed for the harbor or were anchored in the deep water, sleeping.

She rounded the cut and looked for Ash's little shack, which was barely visible in its nest of dunes and pine trees. If she hadn't known it was there, she probably wouldn't have seen it. But Beauty, the big pelican, was there on a stump and he flapped his good wing and sailed off when he heard the boat. A flotilla of seagulls rose from the surf and swooped overhead inquisitively.

"No fish today, children," she told them cheerfully. Taking her at her word, they sailed skyward.

The current in the channel was running fast and Kate was glad to steer the boat out into the gulf, which seemed to take the fast blend of river and sound water to its vast blue bosom and soothe it, as a mother with an obstreperous child.

The slender shaft of the island glowed pearly white. Kate slowed the throttle to admire the sculptured ruffles of white sand embroidered in shells. Sometimes this narrow reach of island was covered by high tide. Some long-ago hurricane had made a gracile cut six or eight feet wide across it and a full tide would rush through it, beaching the empty amber shells of devil crabs. Sometimes when it receded it left a succulent flounder or stone crabs trapped for the taking. Benjy had liked to stretch a seine across this little ditch to trap mullet. And then, chagrined by the unfairness of taking fish that had no sporting chance, he would throw all of them back except a couple to filet for their supper.

Kate smiled at the memory and searched the beach ahead of the bow. Underwater geography was capricious here. You never knew when there would be water enough for even a shallow draft boat. The constant rearranging of the sand made the edges of the wedge uncertain. But there were natural deep-water coves just before the arrowhead began, on both sides of it, if Kate remembered correctly. She decided to anchor there and wade ashore.

She recognized the deep water by its darker color and nosed the little boat shoreward. Island vegetation, nonexistent on the shaft, was rich and luxuriant on the broad high wedge.

Winds had bonsaied the old oaks, twisting them into

whimsical shapes. The pines—virgin, unturpentined growth—were enormous, shading palmettos, yaupon, and swamp myrtle. Kate rounded a thick stand of palmetto at the edge of the cove and saw another boat swinging at anchor. It was black.

She felt a sudden tremor of fear.

It was silly to have any superstition about the color of a boat. But the one that had been there when Sarah Langhorne was consumed by sharks was black. Was this the same one? She started to put the engine in reverse and ease out of the cove when she heard someone calling her name. She pushed the throttle into neutral and looked around. Very close, just beyond the palmettos, she saw Raynor Ellis, the ferryboat captain.

He motioned for her to come ashore. Two other men in elegant yachting outfits materialized at his side.

Now, what are they up to? Kate asked herself. Ray came closer to the water and Kate saw he had a deep-sea fishing rod in his hands. *Oh, well,* she thought, *a charter for tourists.* She steered the boat back into the cove and started to throw the anchor overboard when Ray stepped to the water's edge and said, "Throw me your line. There's a stump here we can tie to."

Kate killed the motor, letting the boat drift in while she uncoiled the line on the bow and threw it to him.

"Come on ashore, Katie, love," said Ray, smiling his sunny Viking smile and extending a hand to her. "I want you to meet some nice folks, here from New York to sample our fish."

The "nice folks" were a fat man with a blistered nose

and a small swarthy man with black sideburns curling up toward his yachting cap. They nodded and smiled as Ray made introductions.

"Count Alexis Bulgay"—the fat man wiped his sausage-shaped fingers and damp meaty palm on his seat before extending a hand to Kate—"and Henry Clay Shenstone"—the wiry, black-eyed man stuck out a long bony hand.

"This is our newspaper lady I told you about," Ray said, indicating Kate.

"Aah," said the fat man, looking at Kate with something akin to interest in his small piggish eyes.

"Count?" Kate said. "A real royal count?"

The fat man seemed disposed to let it pass as truth, but Ray said, "Aw, no. It's his nickname. He hates it, but I let it slip sometimes.

"Come on up on high ground and break bread with us," Ray added. "These gents believe in going well provisioned. They brought a feast from Zabar's, that famous New York deli. Wine and beer, even."

"Are you catching any fish?" Kate asked, looking at all the expensive gear left carelessly lying in the sand.

"Not yet," said Ray. "We've done a little surf casting, but I believe the big ones are out there." He nodded vaguely toward the Yucatán Peninsula. "We're going to tackle them after lunch when the tide is right."

Kate looked at the long black boat and screwed up her courage.

"You got a new boat, Ray?"

"Not me," he said, laughing. "I wouldn't want this old yawl. The count rented it for its seagoing ability.

They don't trust my homey little craft in deep water."

"Where'd you get it, Count?" Kate asked.

The fat man looked vague and shrugged. His dark friend changed the subject by asking if there were any porpoises to be seen around the island.

"Oh, yes!" said Kate. "Lots of them. I'm surprised you haven't already seen schools of them. They like to follow boats through the cut. There's one that follows the ferryboat all the time, isn't there, Ray?"

"Sure is," said the ferryboat captain. "He's my copilot. He comes across with me nearly every day. Visitors love him."

The fat man's mouth dropped open. "Like Flipper? You seen him on TV? He's something!"

"Aw, he's not real," put in Shenstone unexpectedly. "That's all trick photography. They can do that. Use a artificial fish."

The count was outraged. "It is not, goddammit! That's a real fish." He appealed to Ray.

"He is real," Ray said. "A mammal, not a fish, of course. There were five of them in all and some of the people on the island saw them when the movie was being shot."

The fat man was triumphant. The dark one sulked. Kate thought of the phrase "when thieves fall out" and was amused that it could be over Flipper.

But they had brought a good lunch and Kate helped Ray spread a cloth beneath a live oak tree on the highest point of the arrowhead. A dune sheltered them from the north wind, making a small pocket of warmth.

The water there was sapphire, the waves lace-edged.

The wind made music in the pine trees overhead. It was a lovely spot and unspoiled by builders because it was vulnerable to storm winds and too far from the mainland for a comfortable commute, particularly since the ferry didn't come near it and there was no road along the shaft.

Ray filled a plastic glass with wine for Kate despite her objections. "I'm driving," she protested.

"Yeah, but you got a wide road and practically no traffic today," joked Ray.

The wine, a red she had not tasted before, was delicious and Kate made no objection when Shenstone refilled her glass. When they had eaten all the food, the count folded up his navy-blue blazer and made himself comfortable on a pine-needle-carpeted slope for a nap. Shenstone wandered back of a clump of palmettos, probably on a toilet errand, Kate thought.

And then the wine spoke.

"Tell me, Ray, what are they really doing here?"

"I told you," said the blond giant, smiling at her. "Fish."

"More like 'fishy,'" Kate muttered. "I don't for a moment believe that's what they're up to. I think it's something else. And not good. Don't you really know? Or can't you find out?"

"If it will make you feel any better, I'll look into it," said Ray, and then added plaintively, "But you're interfering with my living, you know. I don't investigate every Tom, Dick, and Harry who asks me to take him fishing."

"Most Tom, Dick, and Harrys are obviously all right," Kate said. "These are obviously something else.

Those fancy yachting costumes, leaving their fishing gear in the sand, thinking Flipper is a stuffed fish. Ray, if you don't want to find out about them, I'm going to. We're already having enough trouble on Ila."

"Don't you bother," Ray said. "I'll take care of it. And Kate, it would be helpful if you didn't blat it around till I've had a chance."

Kate grinned. "Well, okay, but I was thinking about having a nice little tea to welcome the count and his friend to Ila Island."

Ray laughed, but mirthlessly, Kate thought, and began picking up the picnic stuff. She helped him and when it was done, she stood up and stretched.

"I'd better start back," she said. "But first I think I'll walk along the beach. It's so beautiful. The best shelling on the gulf."

Ray looked at the sky, which seemed as innocent of turbulent weather signs as the face of a newborn baby.

"I wouldn't delay too long, Kate," he said.

Kate didn't ask if he and his visitors would be shoving off for more fishing. Her attention was drawn to tracks across the brow of the hill, leading to a pine stake. She followed the tracks and there was another— new-sawn pine recently driven into the sand—and beyond that another.

She looked back for Ray, but he and his fishermen had gone from the sunny little picnic spot. Suddenly the beauty of the beach and the bountiful shells held no interest for Kate. She set off for the boat, walking on the wet sand at the edge of the water for better traction and faster progress.

The black boat was missing when she got to the cove, the water still roughened by its wake. She untied the Nobles' boat and jumped in and started the engine. It ran smoothly, and outside the cove she slowed the engine. A few stakes, the isolation of the barb, a couple of men not unlike characters she sometimes ran into on newspaper stories, and the black boat had combined to make a sissy of her, she thought ironically. She had nothing to be afraid of. That decided, she suddenly felt water sloshing around her feet. She looked behind her. The plug was out of the drain in the stern and the gulf was pouring in. Putting the throttle on idle, she hurried to the stern to find the plug that belonged in the drain. If it was there, it was covered with water and she couldn't find it.

If it was there ... *How juvenile*, Kate thought. No grown person would regard removing the plug as particularly serious if the boat was moving. All she had to do was speed up and run the water out of the boat. People did that all the time. Speed would reverse the flow of the water.

Kate revved up the engine and steered the boat into the deep water, keeping as close to the shoreline as she dared. Suddenly the engine coughed, the boat slowed, and she realized she was aground. Water came surging back in through the drain.

Kate found a paddle and stuck it overboard to gauge the depth. She had helped Benjy push their little boat off sand bars in the past. This might not be too tough.

But it was. Without Benjy's strength she did not

seem equal to dislodging the hull. And water kept pouring in. Kate took off her sweater and stuffed it in the
drain. She dived to find the spot where the bottom of
the boat was cleaving to the sand bar. The rudder
seemed to have dug in.

She surfaced and looked toward the shore. It would
be a long swim but with a life jacket not too difficult.
She just couldn't stand to leave Nora's boat to be pum-
meled by waves and either washed out to sea or sunk if
the water continued to pour in.

She dived again and came up to hear a light plane
overhead.

There were flares in the glove compartment, but she
couldn't get to them fast enough. She snatched off her
shirt and flapped it in the air. Whoever it was—and she
wasn't good at recognizing planes—she hoped they
would help her out of the cold water. Her hands were
blue and she suspected the rest of her body was solidify-
ing into a block of ice. A big fish swam close to her and
she shouted and beat the water with her hands.

"Go away!" she cried.

The way she had churned up the bottom, sand
obscured the fish and she could only hope that it was
not a shark. There were other big fish—Flipper types,
even—so why was she acting paranoid? Sharks could be
friendly if you didn't threaten them. *Oh, be friendly,
shark,* she prayed.

The plane dipped a wing at her and raced its engine.
She clung to the boat, her teeth chattering. *Don't go
away, don't go away,* she urged it. And it didn't. The

beach was soft and narrow, but the pilot had evidently gauged the bare, windwept spine of Ila and picked it for a landing.

Kate started swimming for the shore.

Two people met her at the water's edge. Greg Herren and Ash. Greg carried a blanket, which he wrapped around her.

"Oh, I'm glad to see you!" Kate stammered. "How did you know to come?"

"Just riding around," Greg said lightly, putting an arm around her and propelling her up the slope to the plane.

"Me, too," said Ash. "Just riding around with him."

"Liars," said Kate. "You knew I was in trouble!"

"You in trouble?" asked Greg blandly.

Ash snickered. "Look to me like you was in water."

Kate sniffled and accepted a tissue Greg handed her. "I don't want to go off and leave Nora's boat," she said. "It's about all she has left. I was so stupid not to check the drain plug."

"It was all right on the trip out, wasn't it?" Greg asked.

"Oh, yes," Kate said, remembering. "No trouble at all."

"Well, don't worry," Greg said. "I have already radioed for a launch to come and tow it home. We'll fly over it till the launch spots it."

The sun was still high when Kate got back to her house. She had the fire built up and dry clothes on when Mindy and Emmy brought Nora in with her shopping bags.

She looked weary and accepted a cup of coffee.

"Did you get a lot of pretty things?" Kate said.

Nora shook her head. "I made the mistake of going to the bank first. Not enough money in our account for much. I charged a few things. But Kate, I can't imagine ... I just don't know. We had a fair balance. Phil didn't tell me otherwise."

"Oh, honey, I can lend you a few bucks," Kate said.

"I offered to," Mindy said. "But she wanted to stick to what she felt comfortable about. And that's all right. We got enough island clothes, underwear, and one outfit for going to town."

"Which I'm going to have to do soon—to get a job," Nora said.

"There will be insurance money, Nora," Emmy interposed. "The house and Phil's life insurance."

Nora sighed. "The house was insured twenty years ago. What it was worth then and what it will cost to rebuild it now must be vastly different. I don't think Phil's life insurance can be very much. He borrowed on it to buy our third of the island. The papers ..." she faltered, "were in the house."

They were all silent, looking into the fire with helpless sympathy.

"I don't think getting a job in town is such a bad idea," Mindy ventured after a while. "Get your mind off the island. Meet new people. Do something different."

"Which town, what job?" Nora asked, smiling wearily.

Kate hadn't mentioned the near sinking of Nora's boat. She didn't know why she was waiting. Both Mindy and Emmy would learn about it, probably very soon. Some impulse to hold back, she supposed, and that was silly on an island where everybody knew everybody's business. Or did they?

Unexpectedly she said, "Nora, don't you own the arrowhead?"

Nora looked surprised. "I think so," she said. "Most of it, anyhow. Phil thought it was an important refuge for birds. You know ospreys nest there and there are red-tailed hawks and loons. All kinds of birds which we don't have at this end of the arrow. Why do you ask?"

"Well, I was there today. In fact, I shared a picnic with Ray Ellis and some people he had in tow. He said he brought them to fish, but they didn't look like fishermen to me. I wonder if they might be interested in buying the arrowhead from you."

Nora shook her head emphatically. "I wouldn't sell it. Never. Phil was in the process of turning it over to the state environmental agency. That's one thing I can do for him, and I certainly intend to."

Mindy stood up and reached for her jacket. "How did you happen to be on the arrowhead?" she asked idly.

"Oh, just cruising around," Kate said airily. "It's such a beautiful spot. I took an apple and a sandwich and was going to find a spot on the hill, like we used to do."

"And Ray had a group there?"

"Not a group. Two men. New Yorkers, he said, and they did bring a wonderful deli lunch from Zabar's. Incidentally"—she pretended it was an afterthought—"I grounded your boat, Nora, but it's all right. Greg Herren happened to be flying over and he radioed somebody to tow it home."

"Happens all the time," Nora said reassuringly. "You got back safely, I see."

For some reason she didn't understand, Kate didn't want to tell them the whole story—the missing plug, the rapidly sinking boat, the part old Ash played in it. But she did decide to go down to the dock and check on the boat to be sure it had arrived in good order.

Mindy and Emmy left and Nora picked up a book and went in for a nap.

"I'm going to walk to the dock," Kate said. "I think I'll go along the beach."

"It's longer," Nora murmured from her pillow. "But more private. You won't see anybody this time of year and Pepper might get in a swim if it isn't too cold. I'd go with you, but—"

"Oh, shopping does you in," Kate said. "Take a rest and I'll come back and we'll stir up something for supper."

"You're good to me," Nora said. "I couldn't weather this without you. I know something awful is going on and I can't get myself together and dope it out. I'm a coward, Kate. I ought to tell you to go on back to your newspaper and your house, and take charge of my own life." She paused and her blue eyes filled with tears. "What's left of it."

Kate stopped inside the door with her jacket in hand. "Something *is* going on, honey. It might take both of us to dope it out. Why do you think you didn't have any money in the bank, for instance? Was it like Phil to draw it out without telling you?"

Nora shook her head. "Maybe the checking account. We didn't always tell each other about little expenditures. You know, utilities or groceries or something for the airplane or the boat. But Kate"—she pushed her pillow against the headboard and hoisted herself up in bed—"I didn't want to say anything about it to Mindy. She thinks worrying over money is so grubby and tacky. But the savings account was down to nothing. Phil always kept several thousand dollars in that for insurance and taxes and emergencies. It had fifty dollars left. That was all!"

"Did you ask anybody at the bank about his withdrawals?"

"Yes, I did, and Dick Trench, the bank manager, told me Phil drew out several hundred dollars from our checking account and about three thousand from our savings the day he came home from the hospital."

"Did Dick know what for? Did Phil write a check for somebody?"

"It was a cash withdrawal."

"How funny," Kate mused. "He wasn't on the mainland very long and he didn't bring that big wad of cash to the island when he came?"

"I didn't see it and he didn't mention it. And the next morning—well, you know."

Kate thought, *And then he was dead and then there was the funeral and the fire. It could have been in that big desk in the living room. It could have burned up. Poor Nora.*

She drew on her jacket slowly, not looking at Nora but staring out the French door at the incoming tide.

"Well, try not to worry," she said after a moment. "It'll all come clear to us by and by."

Nora smiled and slid back down in the bed, pulling up the blue and white "drunkard's path" quilt Kate had spread over the foot. "There's not a whole lot I can do about it right now, is there?"

Kate went out the door, calling Pepper and wondering if there wasn't something Nora could do if she had more energy and spunk. Maybe she could answer a lot of questions which nagged Kate, but she seemed so fragile. For the first time since Kate had known her, she seemed limp and listless and almost past caring what happened to her. The only thing which produced a show of spirit was the suggestion that she might want to sell her share of the island and move away. That Nora was forcefully against.

The dunes on either side of the little boardwalk to the beach were ornamented with the baby-hand tracks of coons and Kate stopped to trace one in the white sand. The island was full of raccoons, if the marauding feral cats hadn't done them in. They were quiet, nonaggressive animals and when she unexpectedly turned on an outside light at night, she was likely to find one standing up on his haunches looking curiously toward the house, his little black-masked face comic and appealing. She would have liked one for a pet, but Benjy had talked her out of it. They made funny charming pets, he agreed, and also all-out pains in the neck. Nothing in the house would be safe from their capers and they would make the lives of Pepper and Sugar miserable.

Kate gave in. She didn't want to complicate the lives of the in-house family. But she always stopped to admire the little paw prints and always searched the bushes carefully, hoping to see a coon in the daytime. They were nocturnal animals and the only time she had ever seen one in daylight was one afternoon when she and Benjy, weary from working on the house, settled down for a nap. She had seen movement in a pine tree in the woods beyond their driveway. Looking closely, she saw three coons playing together in the treetop. They frolicked like fun-loving children and she and Benjy gave up on their naps and lay quietly a long time looking at them.

When will I stop remembering? she thought, stepping off the end of the walkway into the sand. *When will I stop missing him?* She should be easier on Nora, who had not had time for healing, who had even been deprived of her own special place for licking her wounds.

Kate turned toward what they considered the busy end of the island, the ferry dock, the yacht club, the airstrip. It was a long walk down the beach, past half a dozen houses, through the woods, across a little creek, and then over the landing strip and down to the dock. But it was beautiful in the light of the descending sun. Pepper romped ahead, quite recovered from his injuries, and Kate felt a subtle lifting of her spirits. The tide was coming in, dark blue and musical. Shrimp boats were coming to life in the sound, jeweled galleons setting forth on the sapphire sea.

A flight of home-going pelicans went past her. Seagulls riding the waves rose up and took to the sky. Sandpipers scurried across the white sand, sounding their cheerful "Tileet! Tileet!" cry. The wind stirred in the tawny fronds of sea oats and as she passed the last house, Kate saw the wide tractor-tread tracks of an alligator crossing the beach and disappearing in the bushes toward the marsh. She didn't like alligators, but seeing one lonely track toward a home in the marsh, she remembered Christopher Morley's delight in seeing a whale cavorting in the deep seawater off Cape Cod—"Moby Dick," he had written, "sliding on his own cellar door."

As long as the alligator went home to his own cellar door, she had no quarrel with him. In fact, the island as it was, as it always had been, brought deep content to her. The other barrier islands had been tethered to the coast by bridges with resulting paved roads over the silver sand and coveys of little pink and blue beach houses lined up, cheek-by-jowl, to cut off the view of the water. People and cars and fast-food establishments followed.

Only the one the Seminoles called *Ila* for "arrow" remained tranquil and unspoiled. No, that was wrong. Something evil had come to Ila and she didn't know what it was. Illness and death and natural disasters like storms and the lightning which had struck the Nobles' house could be endured; but she wasn't sure that there was any way to become reconciled to what was happening now.

Suddenly Kate heard the sound of a motor going at a low speed behind her. She turned. Close in, just beyond the shallow water, obviously geared to her pace, was the black boat!

The impulse of beach walkers is to wave at passing craft, sometimes to wade out and accept a ride or a gift of fresh-caught mullet. This time Kate turned sharply to the right and took off through the woods. Pepper saw and turned and was ahead of her.

I won't run, she told herself doggedly. *I'm not afraid. I'm simply going to take the old road.*

But her heart was racing and her feet barely touched the sandy ruts, so fast did she pick them up and put them down. She reached the top of the slope, breathless and aching from the exertion. Hidden by tall beach shrubs, she dared to turn and look back. The boat was moving slowly, but suddenly it swerved north and, gathering speed, headed for the mainland shore.

Relieved and suddenly very tired, Kate sagged down on the pine-needle-carpeted road. Catching her breath, she took off her sneakers and shook the sand out of them.

Silly, she scolded herself when at last she got to her feet. *What could they do to me? What would they want to do to me, a plain, tacky, middle-aged woman?* But, remembering the missing plug from Nora's boat, she decided to stay on the woods road and keep under cover just in case the black boat reversed itself and came back to Ila.

It might have been quicker to stay on the beach and follow the curve of the harbor, but she often took the woods road simply because she liked it. The weathered cypress log foundation of an old turpentiner's shack was still there and a long-ago hurricane had washed in bottles from an abandoned dump somewhere down the coast. She always expected to find a rare and beautiful bottle, but today she didn't linger to look. She headed straight for the footlog across Cowkeeper Creek, named for a famous old Seminole chief, although it was a sluggish, unimpressive stream of footlog dimensions.

She had seen a snake here once and she always looked carefully before she set foot on the log. The small stream was dark and placid. The little white button-topped reeds that children called hatpins flourished along the edge. The bronze swamp myrtle grew close, its blue-black berries ready for picking if Kate ever got around to boiling them down for the gulf coaster's version of bayberry candles. She never had, but she thought about it every winter.

The yaupon, well hidden in thickets of pine and cypress and palmetto, was loaded with red berries the birds would harvest as soon as they saw them. The footlog and little road emerged at the edge of the grassy airstrip. Kate paused to look at it. Not impeccably golf course green, for it had a rough shell and sand base and there was no way of watering it in summer dry spells, but it looked pretty good to Kate. When Old Lady Sanderson abandoned the idea of making Ila a resort, somebody had grazed cattle on the landing strip for a while, presenting a hazard to unwary pilots. With residual cow manure and Phil's devotion to the flying fraternity causing him to sod it and mow it regularly, the little strip was serviceable and really the only swatch of lawn on the island.

Kate cut across it on her way to the boat dock. There were three planes in the parking area—the Nobles', Greg Herren's, and one she didn't recognize. Kate paused to look it over—a snappy little Beechcraft that would accommodate four, maybe six people. It looked brand-new.

She stood admiring it for a moment, wishing that she, too, had such a machine and could fly it. It would certainly make trips to Ila easier than that day-long battle with traffic on I-75. Benjy had flown in the Marines and had his commercial license, but they had never been able to afford a plane of their own. He had to make do with flying in the right seat in police helicopters.

If she had a plane she could get to Simolona and make some phone calls she had begun to feel pressured about.

Kate laid an admiring finger on the blue wing tip, which felt cool and satiny, and went on to the boat dock. She carefully checked over the boats tied up there, trying to match craft to owner, but she mainly looked for a black boat.

It was not there and she chided herself for her wariness. The Seminole Indians had a feeling about the color black, probably because of what they called the "black drink," the draught of death. But it was silly for her to be superstitious about the color of the boat. Would she get nervy like this if it were a blue boat?

Only, she decided, if it were run by New York types

who pretended to be on a deep-sea fishing trip in white flannels, blue blazers, and yachting caps.

She went down to the Nobles' mooring. Their boat was safely tied up, dry of bottom, with a new plug in the stern drain. Greg must have supplied it. He was rapidly winning her approval by being on hand when she needed help. She smiled ruefully, remembering the old neighbor in the country who had admired Benjy's ability to rebuild or repair anything around their log cabin. His accolade had been incorporated into their family vocabulary.

"He's a regular handicap," the farmer had said of Benjy. And now it seemed that Greg, who had come to her aid when Nora's boat was fortuitously delayed from going to the bottom by striking a sandbar, was also a "regular handicap."

Kate walked down to the end of the ferry dock, deserted now, to see the sunset and, remembering that Nora was probably awake and hungry, turned back. Suddenly she heard, from the direction of the little yacht clubhouse beyond acres of dilapidated cars, somebody calling her name.

It was the Bobbsey twins, Debbie and Dabney, speaking in unison.

"Kate! Kate! Wait up!" they shouted together.

Kate walked to meet them.

"Dear children," she said, admiring their identical costumes and their close to identical rosy faces and blond hair. "I thought you had gone to cruise in the Bahamas."

Dab took over. "No, ma'am, our mothers wouldn't let us."

"Your mothers?" Kate repeated, amused. After all, they were grown up and married.

"My mother the most," said Deb. "She said it wasn't nice for us to run out so soon after Philip's death. She said Nora might need us and it was only good manners to be here and stand by."

"So you bought a new plane and came back?"

"Oh, no," Dab said. "We had it on order and happened to get delivery yesterday."

"An old day-old airplane," said Kate, laughing. "You all are terrible! When it gets two weeks old are you going to trade it in?"

They looked sheepish together, identical instant embarrassment. Then they shook their heads together.

Somebody's mother—Kate couldn't be sure who was related to whom—came out from behind a junky old van. She was also a little blonde with close-cropped flaxen hair and blue eyes like Deb's and Dab's, the only difference being a soft bloom of age on her pink face very like the bloom on ripening fruit.

"Ah, Kate," she said softly, "how are you? You look wonderful. It's just lovely to see you again!"

Kate's puzzlement gave way to amusement. It didn't much matter whose mother she was. They were all the same, those two families, equally rich, equally beautiful, equally committed to the open-with-a-compliment credo. She knew she didn't "look wonderful." In fact, she hadn't thought about how she looked in heaven knows when. A little scrub with soap and water, a quick pass with a hairbrush, and she considered herself groomed for the day. But the Winklers (Dab's family) and the Claibornes (Deb's) thought noblesse oblige meant instantly attributing beauty and charm and faultless behavior to one and all.

Part of their creed was to say their own name upon meeting, a charming show of humility suggesting that nobody would remember little old me. False it may be, but when this little woman held out a soft pink hand and said sweetly "Winkie Winkler, remember me?" Kate was grateful.

"Oh, certainly," Kate managed smoothly. "How nice to see you again. You haven't been on the island in quite some time, have you?"

"Ages," said Winkie while Kate racked her brain to identify her more accurately. Her real name was something like Annie Mae or Rosa Dee and she was Dab's mother. Dabney Winkler, of course.

"The children—all of us—are so distressed over losing that wonderful man. And their house—how cruel! I told Dabney we must all be as supportive as possible to his wife."

Supportive—a fad word, thought Kate. *Does it mean sympathy or a nice fat loan to rebuild?* She smiled and nodded and wondered if she should invite them all back to her house for supper.

"Nora's at my house," she persuaded herself to say. "Why don't you all come and we'll make a sandwich or something?"

"How very gracious of you," said Winkie.

"You sweet thing!" cried Deb, and she and Dab, one on either side, gave Kate a joint hug.

Kate interpreted it as acceptance and wondered what on earth she would feed them.

She needn't have worried. Deb and Dab had a Porsche, almost as shiny as their airplane, brought to the island when they bought their house. They had already loaded it with boxes of groceries, topped by an Abercrombie & Fitch picnic basket packed with cold meats and fancy breads.

"We'll just run this grub down to your house and come back for you and Mom," Dab said.

Kate and Winkie nodded and smiled and started walking slowly down the beach road. Such deprivation, Kate was thinking, a two-seat car, not nearly as accommodating and commodious as her old wreck. Oh, the sufferings of the rich!

And then Winkie, dropping her saccharine manner, said briskly, "Now tell me, who killed him?"

9

►Kate looked at Winkie Winkler thoughtfully. What did this little pink and gold woman know about Phil's death?

"You heard that he was killed?" she finally said.

"Stands to reason," Winkie said. "And their house … I bet that was arson."

Kate hesitated. "I don't know. I'd be glad if you have any information or ideas. I told Nora I'd help her look into it."

"Oke, I'll help you," said Winkie. "I read a lot of murder mysteries. First, who hated Phil?"

"Oh, nobody could hate Phil!" Kate protested. "Everybody I know really cared about him."

"Oke," said Winkie again. "Then he must have had something that somebody wanted ba-ad!"

Kate was spared from answering by a faint *meow* from the landing strip. She and Winkie stopped and looked.

Old Graymalkin came out of a clump of bushes.

"Well, Gray," said Kate, going toward her. "Where have you been?"

"Pussy, pussy!" said Winkie in her high sweet voice.

Kate thought a look of distaste passed over the feline countenance. Graymalkin was a dignified elderly cat. She was not accustomed to nicknames and to be called the generic "pussy" instead of by her fine Shakespearean name was an affront.

Kate picked her up and stroked her silky fur, pulling off leaves and a bramble.

"Your mama will be glad to see you," she whispered to the old cat.

Dab returned with the Porsche and managed to wedge the two women and the cat into its sleek and elegant confines.

Nora was immoderately glad to see Graymalkin. She greeted Winkie politely enough and she had been helping Deb set out the food and had put on a pot of coffee, but when Kate thrust the old cat into her arms, Nora laughed and cried and collapsed into a rocker, clutching Graymalkin to her breast.

"You crazy wandering beast," she murmured, her face buried in the gray cat hair. "Where did you go? Are you hungry? Have you had fresh water?" She appealed to Kate. "You won't mind if she stays with us, will you?"

"Honored," said Kate. "Even Pepper likes Graymalkin."

Nora made a face. "Let's say he respects her ... her sharp claws. But if you're sure it's no imposition, I'm going to find a brush and clean her up and feed her and she can sleep on my bed tonight."

She disappeared into the guest room with Graymalkin in her arms.

"She better watch it," murmured Winkie. "A woman alone can get an obsession about a cat. Old maids and widows always do that."

"Mother-r!" protested Deb. "Nora's not like that. Graymalkin's just all the family she has left."

"See what I mean?" said Winkie triumphantly.

Kate changed the subject.

"You know, I'm crazy to take a ride in that new plane of yours," she said to Dab. "How would you feel about running me over to Simolona tomorrow?"

Dab slowed down his mastication of a pastrami sandwich to beam at Kate.

"Nothing I'd like better," he said. "You can even fly it, if you want to."

"Thank you, but no thank you," Kate said. "I fly Delta. But there are several things I want to do in Simolona and if you really don't mind, you could drop me off at that little strip north of town. You know the one near the dump?"

Dab did know and he would be inordinately delighted to meet Kate—and Nora, if she cared to go—at the landing strip the next morning, weather permitting.

The weather did permit—cool and clear and windless. Deb and Winkie elected to stay behind to catch up on their sleep and Nora, pleased to have Graymalkin back, decided to stay behind and give Kate's house the cleaning she hadn't had time for.

The ten-mile flight took minutes. Dab landed his smart little ship on the dewy grass strip where the smell of Simolona's dump was redolent in the soft morning air. Assured by Kate that she would get a ride into town, he took off again. Kate walked in the direction of the highway and was overtaken just as she reached it by the town's garbage truck.

"Going my way?" called Sam Busby, the long-time driver.

"I sure hope so," said Kate. "You headed for town?"

"Town and all that good stuff the ladies of Simolona set out by their back steps for me."

Kate laughed. "I know it's pretty fragrant, with all the seafood leavings people have here."

"Evening in Paris," said Sam.

Sam deposited her in front of the drugstore.

"Come in and I'll buy you a cup of coffee," Kate offered.

"Oka-ay!" cried Sam. "Let me park this here Mercedes and I'll be right in."

There was already a sizable crowd at Doc Joe's soda fountain, some Kate knew, most she didn't know. They edged over to make room for her and Sam, and Doc's waitress Merleen took her order and slid two cups of coffee in front of them. Nobody made any introductions and conversation was speedily resumed.

"You gon' git 'em out, Colonel?" one of the men asked the only suited and tied member of the group. Kate took him to be the other lawyer in town, since the old-time title for any member of the legal profession was "Colonel."

"They're entitled to bail," the lawyer said.

"Wouldn't be if I was the judge," muttered a shrimp fisherman Kate half recognized. "They bad news."

"Who they talking about?" Kate whispered to Sam Busby as he took the stool beside her and reached for his coffee.

"Simolona's criminal element," said Sam. "Only Mafia we got."

"We so low on criminals around here," said Merleen with obvious dissatisfaction, "we got to depend on the Pinson boys."

"Yep," said another fisherman. "They do the best they can. Always stealing gas, taking anything that's not welded on. What did they take this time, Colonel?"

"Why, they haven't been found guilty of taking anything," said the young lawyer pompously.

"Ain't talking about found guilty," said the fisherman. "Talking about what the law was lucky enough to catch 'em at."

"You could check with the sheriff," said the lawyer blandly, reaching up to put his quarter on the cash register. "I must be on my way."

"I must be on my way," mimicked an old fellow in rubber boots and a plaid windbreaker.

"He ain't gon' tell you nothing," said Merleen.

"As if we didn't all know," put in another. "This time it wasn't just gas. It was a boat. Belonged to that feller runs the motel over on the river. Lige Roan."

"They stole a boat?" asked Doc Joe, who had joined

Merleen back of the counter. "That's serious. Stealing a boat around here is like stealing a horse in the Old West. Hanging offense."

He smiled around at the fishermen, indicating it was a joke, but they didn't seem amused.

"Can be a man's living," muttered one.

"Bail on that will be high," the old man in the boots offered. "Big larceny."

"And their daddy ain't here to git 'em out," said Merleen happily. "Gone to take his new girlfriend to Disney World."

"The father's girlfriend?" Kate whispered to Sam.

He nodded cheerfully. "Old man's a hell-raiser. Wife's dead, but he ain't—not by a long shot!"

Kate stood up. She hadn't sized up Winkie Dabney as a mental giant, but the points she made about Phil Noble's death were simple and direct and absolutely on track.

Who hated him? The only person she had heard of was a man named Pinson, probably the gentleman who was even now disporting with his girlfriend at Disney World. But what about his sons? She paid for her and Sam's coffee, thanked him again for the ride, and climbed the stairs to Cecil James's office.

Again he had no secretary in the outer office. Again he did obeisance to his computer. But when Kate spoke to him from the door, he hurried forward to greet her, hand outstretched.

"I want to go over to the Franklin County Jail and talk to those Pinson boys," Kate said without preamble. "Can you go with me? I don't mean as a lawyer," she added hastily. "I mean for the ride and somebody to talk about Phil Noble."

"As it happens, Al Shadducks asked me to see about getting bond for them," the young lawyer said. "He has a hearing in Tallahassee and he said the old man would have his head if he let those boys stay in jail. We can go over together."

"Would you let me talk to them?"

"I don't think that would be proper," James said firmly. "I am in effect representing them in Al's place and I don't think your interest is friendly."

"Damn right it's not," said Kate emphatically. "I think those kids had something to do with all the hideous happenings on Ila. Their old man hated Phil and the kids were probably fed his venom with their mother's milk. I believe they surrounded Phil with snakes, for a start."

"It's boat stealing they're charged with," said James stiffly.

"That, too," said Kate. "Lige Roan's Boston whaler has been stolen before and was on the scene when Sarah Langhorne was lured to her death. It was also right there when somebody attempted to scuttle Nora's boat and either drown me or leave me to sharks, too. I *need* to talk to those young hoodlums! By the way, how old are they?"

"I think Beau is eighteen, Baze a little older but sort of retarded."

"Not juveniles, then."

James shook his head regretfully.

He rearranged the papers in his briefcase and led

Kate toward the door. He was parked back of the drug-store where Kate had parked when she had arrived in Simolona—oh, how many days ago? She had lost count of time.

"Your car or mine?" she asked.

James looked at her car, with the wrinkles of age on its faded surface, and said promptly "I'll drive," opening the door to a jaunty bright red convertible.

"Nice," said Kate. "The law business in Simolona must be flourishing."

He shook his head. "Graduation gift from my par-ents."

Oh, young, thought Kate. *So young. Everybody's young but me.*

A mile or so down the road she said, "Cecil, if you don't think I should talk to those boys, how about the district attorney?"

"That's up to you," James said. "I don't know where you'll find him today. Not much crime around here. He lives up the river and fishes a lot."

James parked near the jail and went off in the direc-tion of the courthouse or maybe a professional bonds-man, Kate wasn't sure which. She hurried into the jail. A sleepy old gentleman in a khaki uniform looked up from the weekly newspaper he was reading and greeted her cordially. She took a seat where she could see the cell block. In one cell a man slept. In the other the two Pin-son boys sprawled on a double-decker bunk, yawning and sighing noisily and occasionally breaking out in some mournful song. She scraped the legs of the plastic chair on the concrete floor and one of the boys came to attention.

"Ha, a woman!" he said to his brother, who sat up and looked through the bars at Kate.

"That ain't no woman, that's old Kate Mulcay," said the one Kate hoped was Baze and feebleminded.

"Hey, you come to git us out?" Beau smiled ingratiatingly and smoothed his long greasy hair with both hands.

"Well, yeah, we came to get you out," Kate decided, suddenly devious. "At least Mr. James is arranging bond and I came with him. You ready, I reckon?"

"Hell, I *been* ready," said Beau. "This ain't no Holiday Inn."

The old man at the desk shook his newspaper but said nothing.

"All we done," said Baze, "was borry that old boat. We got a better boat than that one ourselves. Old Lige wasn't there to do business with, so we borried it."

"You had somebody wanted to rent it?" asked Kate.

"Shore did," said Baze complacently. "Paid us a-plenty."

"Shut up, sumbitch!" growled Beau.

"Aw, well," said Kate soothingly, "if you returned it ..."

"We tied it up to a dock up the river. That ain't no crime, is it?" said Baze.

"Not like stealing," Kate said. "That's where you put it last time, huh?"

Baze, who was on the top deck, started to answer,

but Beau kicked the mattress and springs so hard it jostled him to the ceiling.

"Damn you!" yelled Baze, and jumped to the floor and started pummeling his brother.

The two young men were dirty and smelly and had the minds and morals of cretins, Kate thought, feeling a little sick. But she compelled herself to get to her feet and walk closer to the cell block. The officer at the desk rattled his paper and peered at her over the top. She glanced out the window and saw Cecil James crossing the street and heading toward the jail. She hurried.

"You boys ain't scared of much, are you?" she said softly.

They stopped hitting one another and looked at her.

"Whatta you mean?" asked Beau.

"Oh," said Kate airily, "I was thinking of getting a couple of nice rattlesnakes for a friend of mine up in Georgia. I'm scared of the things. You ever trap 'em?"

"Shit!" exploded Baze. "All the time!" And then craftily, "What you pay?"

Kate heard James on the steps and lowered her voice to a whisper. "Whatever you charge. What did you get last time?"

Baze was about to say something, but Cecil James was suddenly in the room, glaring at Kate. He handed the officer a piece of paper and walked over to the cell door.

"Morning, boys," he said politely. "You ready to go home?"

"We ain't got a car," said Beau. "You give us a ride?"

James looked reluctant, but he said, "Okay. But no talk, now, you hear me?"

"We know," said Beau grumpily. "We been here before. You don't say nothing to nobody."

"Especially," said James, looking at Kate, "not to ladies who work for newspapers and—"

"Find a wild cat in their house and their dog cut up," Kate put in swiftly.

"Was that your house?" Baze asked. "I thought that one burned down...."

Kate smiled at Cecil and followed along with the boys to his car.

"You double-crossed me," Cecil muttered to Kate as he got in and started the car. "I told you you couldn't talk to them."

"You didn't want me to sit there in grim silence, did you? All I did was pass the time of day." She winked at Baze, who blinked both eyes back.

"When Al Shadducks gets back, you are welcome to them. If they want to confess to stealing that boat, that's between you and him."

"They already have," said Kate, smiling smugly. "'Borry' is their word."

"Now you're working on cats," said Cecil helplessly.

"And snakes," said Kate helpfully.

"Oh, my God!" cried the young lawyer. "I'm going to be disbarred."

"You should choose what our former governor up in Georgia, Lester Maddox, yearned for—a better class of criminals," murmured Kate.

The boys got out at a pink stucco chalet facing the bay. It was planted with pink and white azaleas just coming into bloom and had a full menagerie of concrete birds and animals leading down to a small dock, where a thirty-foot cabin cruiser and a little launch were tied up.

"Pinson boats?" Kate asked.

"Their father's," said James.

"Particular about who uses them, huh? So the boys have to 'borry' from Lige Roan?"

James bit his lip and said nothing.

"Well, it would be dumb to use their own boat or even rent it out for murder and criminal mischief," Kate mused. "Naturally, they had to 'borry.'"

"Can I let you out at your car?" James asked politely.

"If you feel like you can spare my illuminating company," said Kate. "I would like to use your phone, if it's convenient. The pay station at the grocery store always has a line of teenagers waiting."

"The door is unlocked. Help yourself. I have some errands to do."

Kate didn't go to the telephone. She went to the little balcony with its plastic chairs and telescope. She knew she was early, but she wanted to get the feel of the telescope, adjust it to her eyes and to distant people and things.

The big tube on its spindly legs turned easily and Kate swung it back and forth over the little Simolona harbor, turning a knob to focus on a shrimp boat which was coming in and then to the public ramp, where two men in a truck were maneuvering a boat trailer to get a big skiff in the water. Carefully she inched the glass toward the ferry dock. There was no activity there at this time of the week except for the raucous dipping and swirling of the laughing gulls. A boat shed beyond the dock caught the sun on its tin roof, where dew or spray from the river glistened like diamonds. The interior of the shed was in shadow and apparently deserted. Kate waited.

Young Bert pedaled up on a bicycle and took a tackle box and a rod from its basket before he leaned it against a palm tree in the little park. Kate watched as he fiddled with a plug and began casting, throwing his line in easy, graceful arcs.

The sun was climbing and shadows in the darkness of the shed deepened. Kate waited.

Occasionally a truck passed and a home-returning school bus lumbered by. Kate wondered about the time and wished she had brought a cup of coffee from Doc Joe's downstairs.

Maybe she had been wrong, she thought in disgust. Winkie's naive questions—Who hated Phil? Who had the opportunity? Who would profit by his death?—were simplistic. It was evidently going to be more complicated than she thought.

Idly she swung the telescope toward the closed canning plant across the harbor, the one Pinson had bought and shut down. Past it out toward the mouth of the harbor the winter-gold marsh caught the sun. A couple in a skiff were anchored at the edge of the marsh, hunched over in the timeless stance of patient fishermen. She watched them a moment and saw no movement. They and their fishing poles seemed frozen—bees caught in amber.

The river water was brown glass, no boats coming in, no boats going out. Suddenly a pickup truck emerged from behind the old canning factory across the harbor and moved on past the marsh. The road there was soggy and almost obscured by the waving fronds of sea oats. Kate wiggled the knob on the telescope and pushed her eye into it as if she could will herself closer, her view clearer. The truck vanished and reappeared as the marsh vegetation varied from thick to thin and scraggly. It stopped well back from the point where a harbor marker on four sturdy timber legs faced out to sea.

Somebody got out and walked down to the edge of the water, and then Kate saw a boat screened by a growth of young willow trees very close to the shore.

She waited, her eye glued to the glass, hoping it would move out so she could get a good look at it, maybe even focus on its name.

Her hand on the telescope was damp. Her eyes without their customary horn-rimmed glasses blurred. But she clung on, waiting.

Then Cecil James walked in.

"Mrs. Mulcay, are you spying on my neighbors?" he asked affably.

"Just admiring the morning," Kate said. "And looking for a ride back to the island. You wouldn't happen to be going that way, would you? There's not an island boat anywhere down there that I can see."

"As it happens I have some business to transact with Mrs. Noble," he said. "I can give you a ride."

"Fine!" cried Kate. "I can go now. Can you?"

James looked at her, surprised at her enthusiasm, but nodded and picked up more papers and put them in his briefcase. Kate rushed ahead of him, down the stairs, across the street, and along the river to the shed where his boat was moored. She let him pass when they came even with Bert.

"Bert," she said urgently, pausing beside the willow tree where the youngster lounged in the shade. "Did you see a truck go by over there by the cannery?"

"Yes, ma'am," he said. "Beau Pinson's pickup."

"How about out at the mouth of the harbor? Did you see a boat out there?"

"Nothing but a skiff. Somebody pole fishing."

Disappointed, Kate realized he didn't really have a clear view, and she thanked him and galloped to catch up with James.

"You in a right big rush, aren't you?" the young lawyer asked.

"I sure am," Kate said. "How fast can you get to that buoy? If I can just see that boat around the point out there, I'll know for sure—"

She stopped. She didn't really know Cecil James. So far he had been a foot-dragger. She wasn't ready to tell him what she now firmly believed about the happenings on Ila.

There really was no hope of speed from James. He was an old-maidish putterer. He lifted a seat cushion in his launch and carefully stowed his briefcase in there. He took off his suit coat, methodically folding it and tucking it in a plastic case. He donned a nylon jacket and a Greek fisherman's-type cap. He took off his glasses, wiped them with a handkerchief, and put them in a neat little case he apparently kept for the purpose on the dashboard. He replaced them with black Polaroid glasses, which he took off and wiped twice. Then he started checking the boat's gas tank and its engine.

Kate, fidgeting on the dock, sighed and gave up. He was not going to move—and the boat out there around the bend would be gone.

"If we hurried ..." she prodded.

James smiled tolerantly.

"It's not good practice to be in a hurry with a boat," he said. "I always check everything."

Kate sniffed. *Coats and caps and Polaroid glasses,* she thought, but resigned herself to unhitching the bowline and then the stern line. As she could have anticipated, James checked the lines she had coiled on the deck of the launch and rearranged them.

All boats operated at a low speed inside the harbor until they reached the no-wake sign which faced out to sea. This was for the protection of the small craft, which could be swamped by the turbulent wake of a bigger boat. Kate couldn't criticize James for his pokiness in the harbor. It was the law, and by the time they reached the mouth of the river it didn't matter anyhow. The boat she had seen at the point was a speck in the distance.

* * *

A stir of activity greeted them as James's boat, slowed again to no-wake pace, approached the Ila dock.

Deb and Dab rushed up, hand in hand, to tell Kate that Winkie had persuaded Nora to take a little run with them down the coast to picturesque Cedar Key to have an early dinner at what Deb assured Kate was "this too utterly adorable" restaurant.

"I'll get them back before dark," said Dab.

Nora, following slowly behind them, smiled at Kate wanly. "Your house has had a lick and a promise," she said. "I thought I might as well go. It's something to do."

"Good idea," said Kate, putting an arm around her shoulders.

She walked with them a little way toward the landing strip, where Dab was already moving around his plane, checking its vital signs. She wished vaguely that she could keep Nora back and pin her down on several points she now knew contributed to Phil's death. But her talks with Nora up to now had yielded little but grief and hopelessness and anger. What she needed was facts.

She put a hand on Nora's arm to slow her down and let Winkie, radiant in pink and blue and white, get ahead.

"Be thinking," she said. "I think I know what's happening here—almost. But I need some more information. Was there a coroner's report on Finley Sawyer and Paul Lewis?"

Nora glanced ahead at the Winklers, who stood by the plane waiting for her. "Greg's gone to check on that," she said softly. "And some other things. He's got some ideas, too. Talk to him."

Kate nodded and stood back out of the little plane's slipstream.

Cecil James arrived with his briefcase, looking miffed.

"I came to see you, Nora," he said accusingly. "We've got to probate Phil's will and there are things for you to sign about the insurance."

Kate figured he had been slow to catch up with them because he had lingered to tie up his boat with his best Boy Scout knots and then had to change to his jacket, remove his fisherman's cap, and comb his hair and tie his tie.

Nora was smiling at him. "Give me the papers. I'll take them along and sign as we travel. Maybe Dab will let me drop them off in Simolona on the way back."

"Sure," said Winkie cheerfully. "Look out for a cute little parachute."

Cecil James gaped at her in amazement. He had come to be a lawyer and Nora was treating his errand as if it were a grocery list. He clung to his briefcase.

"Aw, open up, you cute thing!" said Winkie roguishly, grabbing the briefcase. "Show me the dotted lines and I'll see that Nora puts her John Henry by every X. We'll get everything back to you pronto. Or would you like to go to Cedar Key with us?"

She had apparently decided that he was in truth a "cute thing" they should have along. He looked uncertainly at the airplane and Dab's arm out the cockpit window impatiently beckoning his passengers with a boarding-time sign. James made a spur of the moment decision—maybe the first he had ever made, Kate thought.

"Are you sure there's room?" He eyed the gleaming fuselage.

"Plenty," said Winkie blithely. "Six passengers and then some. Come on." She linked an arm in his and led the way to the plane.

Kate watched them go in amusement and then she turned to look for Greg Herren's plane. It was missing. The only aircraft left on the parking area was the Nobles' little Cessna 150. Even the boat dock seemed wintertime, midweek empty. The ferry was not due until Friday afternoon. The big sailboat which had been visiting was gone. The Prestons had apparently departed in their little boat, taking Dr. Wells with them.

10

It seemed a good time to sort things out, Kate thought. She would start with Ash.

One if by land, two if by sea? she asked herself à la Paul Revere, trying to decide whether to attempt the soft sand road in her car or to take Nora's boat. She settled on the boat. It started promptly and she felt that for once it was actually gliding over the quiet water. Except for a tug towing a barge and some mullet fishermen throwing a cast net from a skiff in a little inlet, the sound was deserted. Kate waited to turn up the throttle for the pleasure of enjoying the peacefulness. *It may be the last place in Florida where there are no filling stations or Pizza Huts,* she thought contentedly. *Pray Lord that we can keep it that way.*

She made good time getting to the end of the island, only slowing to look at her own house. Pepper, sleeping in the sun on the little boardwalk, raised his head and flapped his tail, apparently with no desire to join her. *He's become a sissy,* she thought indulgently. *A swim in cold water is not for him.* She waved and pushed the throttle forward.

Across the channel she saw a school of porpoises leaping and plunging in formation, and closer to the shore she saw a baby shark nosed into the beach.

"I hope your parents have gone to the mall," she said cheerfully—and then wondered at herself. Evil forces at work all around her, and here she was luxuriating in the beauty of the day and chatting up a baby shark. The pall of gloom and foreboding which had hovered over her for days had not lifted exactly, but there seemed to be a rent in it through which she could see light.

It's because, she told herself, *I know who is at the bottom of our troubles. Or do I?*

She rounded the point and beached the boat, counting on the incoming tide to help her launch it when she was ready to leave. Beauty was not on his customary stump, but Kate thought she saw him diving, one-wingedly, for a fish a little way out.

Ash came limping down the slope to meet her.

"Hidy-do, Kate," he said, but without his customary bounce, Kate thought. His old face looked grayer and saggier than usual and there was a cut on one cheek, red and jaggedly emerging from his whiskers.

Kate waited until he had led the way to his yard fire and pushed a chair toward her. "Okay, Ash," she said. "It's time to level. I think I know something now about the bastard who's trying to kill us off and take the island. But you've got to help me straighten it all out. By the way, who hit you?"

"Hit me?" said Ash. "Where you git that idy?"

"Your face, Ash. Haven't you got a mirror? Have you seen that cut?"

Ash put a dirty paw up to his cheek and then withdrew it. "Aw, Kate," he said, striving for a laugh that didn't come off. "Cut myself shaving."

"All right," said Kate. "Try to joke and put me off about that. Nora's got a first-aid kit in the boat and before I go, I'm going to clean and bandage that cut. In the meantime, who did it?"

"Some fellers want me to move off the island," the old man said in a low tone, ducking his head. "Gimme a day before they come back and burn my house."

Kate looked at the house and her heart sank. Things were worse than she thought if they would attack an old man and his wonderful, terrible stayplace that was as much a part of the island as Beauty, the crippled pelican, the wondrous sunsets, and the majestic storms.

"Who?" said Kate.

"They didn't give no names," mumbled Ash.

"You know who sent them, don't you?"

"I reckon," said the old man tiredly.

Kate took a different tack. "Yesterday when you came with Greg Herren to get me out on the arrowhead, how did that come about? You weren't 'just riding around,' I know."

"I see just about evvabody passes out there in the cut," Ash said defensively. "I seen that black boat and then I seen you go by. I knowed hit was harm a-brewing. I couldn't git to the dock fast enough to tell it, but Greg

Herren's rented house on the gulf ain't too fur to walk in a hurry. I run."

"Well, I didn't thank you properly," Kate said, standing up. "I'm thanking you now. You might have saved my life."

"Could be," said Ash, averting his bedraggled old face. "Them's mean people."

"Ash, I want you to go with me. I'll put something on that cut on your face and we'll radio for help. The Marine Patrol will relay to the sheriff and somebody will come, I know."

Ash looked anxiously at his house and his little fire. His rheumy old eyes sought Beauty, who had returned to his stump. He put out a foot and scuffed sand off a pair of plastic bottles, which, half buried in the sand, outlined his walk.

Kate could see in his hesitation a farewell to his stayplace. He thought that if he left, it would be destroyed. And it might, anyhow.

"If you don't want to go ..." she began gently.

Ash pulled back his shoulders, spit tobacco juice into the fire, and said sturdily, "I'll go, Kate. Hit's murder, ain't hit?"

"It's murder," said Kate.

The radio in the Nobles' boat didn't work. Kate couldn't remember if it ever had. They had relied on the one on Phil's desk, now gone forever in the fire. It may have been that they brought a portable with them when they used the boat. Her own had been put out of commission at the time of the storm. She supposed the batteries were dead. It was a cinch Ash would know nothing about a radio. He considered such contraptions devices of the devil.

She opened up the throttle and pushed the little boat for all it was worth, not even slowing down to diminish the wake when she hit the harbor. There were no boats there, anyhow, she thought. But that was wrong. A new boat had arrived. She stood up to look at it.

"Is that Raynor Ellis's boat?" she asked Ash.

He hitched up his overalls, which dropped damply, and spat into the blue water.

"Hit is," he said.

"Ash, you tie up!" she said. "I'm going to find a radio. Hurry!"

She raced down the dock, looking desperately for a boat that might have a marine radio. Then, catching herself in what she realized was the ultimate stupidity, she turned back to Ellis's boat. Of course, he would have one. A boat that had bunks and a stove and a head would certainly have all the other amenities, particularly the safety devices. But the cabin door was securely locked.

Phil's plane was there, but Kate remembered well Benjy's saying that you couldn't get anybody on that channel until you were fifteen hundred feet in the air.

"Oh, God," she whispered. "He's on the island and there's no way we can call for help."

Mindy! Mindy was still on the island. She could fly the airplane and summon help!

Ash had paused to pick up a long-handled crab scoop net which somebody had left on the dock. *He's going crabbing at a time like this,* Kate thought hysterically. And then a more hysterical idea hit her. He was clutching the handle midway like a club. He intended to use it for self-defense.

Her eyes softened looking at the anxious, threatened, valiant old man in his droopy overalls plodding along grasping a crab net.

"Come on, Ash," she said. "We'll find Mindy."

"Miss Mindy," said the old man hesitantly, "she may not be the best for this. She is sweet on him."

"What did you say?" asked Kate, pausing and turning to stare at him.

"Hit ain't right for me to say this," Ash began.

"To hell with that!" cried Kate. "This is no time for saltwater chivalry! Tell me what you know!"

"That's the trouble. Knowing ain't in hit. I jes' figger from what I've seen that Miss Mindy thinks he's her feller."

"And he's not!" said Kate positively.

"No'm," said Ash sadly. "Not specifically."

"Oh, Ash." Kate wanted to laugh. *Not specifically* was a fine term for arrant duplicity and hanky-panky. "Let's go see Mindy, anyhow. She's a friend. When we tell her what we know, she'll be with us."

Ash said nothing but followed her docilely up the path to Mindy's back door. Kate didn't bother to knock but rushed in, calling her friend's name.

Mindy didn't seem to hear. She sat across the kitchen table from Raynor Ellis, her beautiful dark eyes fixed on his face. Whatever he was saying, he stopped when Kate, followed by Ash, burst into the room.

"What is this?" he asked icily, standing up.

"I'm going to tell you, Ray," Kate said. "I think you

would appreciate knowing before the sheriff gets here. You might want to get off the island."

"Old Katie, playing girl copper again!" Ray said contemptuously. "And what makes you think I would run from the sheriff?"

"Murder," said Kate far more calmly than she felt. She wondered if he could tell she was bluffing.

"Murder?" breathed Mindy as if she had never heard the word before.

"He hired the Pinson boys to put the snakes in Phil's room and in his airplane," Kate said more positively than she felt. "I saw the payoff this morning with the telescope on Cecil James's balcony."

"Shit!" cried Ray. "You couldn't have seen that! Why, the point is covered with trees! That's ridiculous!"

Kate sighed inwardly with relief. He was as good as admitting it. She hadn't mentioned the point. Mindy was staring at him, pale, barely breathing.

"You would do that to Philip Noble?" she whispered at last.

"Of course not! She's fantasizing."

"The wild cat in my house, the fire we thought the lightning set, the attack on my dog," Kate went on relentlessly. "The Pinson boys thought it was all a big joke."

"Oh, my God!" whispered Mindy, pulling out the table drawer and picking up a napkin to wipe her face. Kate, standing beside her, saw an old pistol she had seen before, never once thinking it might be loaded or workable. Mindy's hand hovered over it a second and then she half closed the drawer.

"The Pinsons are crazed on drugs and are mental defectives," said Ray. "If they told you that, they're liars."

"Finley Sawyer, Paul Lewis," Kate went on, pushing her luck. "Environmentalists bent on saving the island. Very mysteriously dead just as you and your New York friends made a last-minute push to take it over."

Mindy looked at him steadily, her black eyes glittering. "I didn't know. ..." she said softly. "Ray, I didn't know. Was it all just to get the land? We could have waited and bought the land!"

We? Kate thought incredulously. *Mindy said "we." Was she in on it, too?*

"Mindy," she said chokily. "I can't believe ... not you, too?"

Mindy laughed harshly. "Not murder ... no! I was helping Ray and the others with a plan to develop the island. A gambling casino on the arrowhead. ... Kate, it would make a lot of money!"

"Gambling casinos are against the law in Florida," Kate objected numbly.

"Arrowhead," gloated Ray. "In case you didn't know, Miss Smart Journalist, the arrowhead is beyond the twelve-mile limit!"

"International waters," said Mindy. "All it would take would be a bulldozer to cut the islands well apart out there where there's already a big cut."

Kate had a feeling she was losing ground. She didn't think their idea would work, but she didn't want to engage in a legalistic maritime law argument with Ray. She wanted him to confess and go.

"And this island?" she asked.

"Hotels," said Mindy in a low voice. "Beautiful big luxury hotels. It could be gorgeous."

"For gamblers," Kate said flatly.

"Gamblers have money," said Ray. "And that's what my partner and I are interested in."

He smiled winningly at Mindy, all white teeth, green eyes, and coin-bright hair. Kate thought she saw Mindy's colorless lips tremble. Her eyes closed briefly and when she opened them they fastened on Ray's gorgeous face. *She's softening,* Kate thought. *She does love him. She will try to protect him.*

Ash, who had been standing behind her with his crab net, suddenly spoke.

"The little girl, Cap'n. She didn't have nothing to do with gambling and hotels and sich."

"She was just pregnant and expected you to marry her," Kate put in.

Mindy looked first at Kate and Ash, then back at Ray.

"Sarah Langhorne," she whispered. "You were sleeping with her? You killed her?"

"Set in the boat and watched her tore up by sharks," said Ash.

"You can't prove that!" cried Ray.

"Yessir, I was a plumb eyewitness," said Ash. "God help me, I hung back when I shoulda went for-ard."

"Shit, you don't even know she's dead. She's probably a runaway. If she died, there would be a body!"

"There is," Kate said.

Mindy was on her feet, pulling open the drawer and reaching for the old pistol.

"You bastard," she said softly.

Ray was also on his feet and he had a gun in his hand, and he was aiming at Kate. Later she thought they must have fired simultaneously.

Ray plummeted to the floor, his shirt front a spreading river of blood, his face and head grotesquely swathed in crab net. Mindy let out a cry and sank back into the chair, her hands still holding the gun and trying to cover her face. Blood was seeping through the front of her sweatshirt.

Kate looked from Ray to Ash. "What ... what did you do?"

"Lord, god, Kate my aim was off! I was a-reaching for his gun hand with my crab net but I got his head instid!"

"You saved my life, I think," And then kneeling beside Mindy, "Maybe hers as well. At least, she's still alive."

Blood was gushing out faster now. "Chest," gasped Mindy. "Ray. Is he ...?

Ash, disentangling his crab net from the ferryboat captain's head, managed the word without regret or triumph: "Dead."

Mindy shivered and a sob rose up in her throat.

"I loved him ... I didn't know ... we were going to be ... married ..."

"Ash, bring towels," Kate cried, frantic at the sight of blood coming faster. And then, to save time, she ran to the linen closet herself and came back, tearing a sheet to strips to clamp a bath towel to Mindy's chest.

"Is the pain awful?" she asked. "Have you got anything for it besides aspirin?"

"Brandy," gasped Mindy, struggling to breathe. The room was smoky, from the shooting, Kate supposed.

"Open windows, Ash," she said quickly. "And don't touch Ray or his gun. Maybe a sheet. Here ..." She handed him the one she had been tearing into bandages. "Cover him up."

She searched the cupboard and came up with the bottle of brandy she had brought Mindy two days ago, now considerably depleted. There was one, maybe two, fingers left and she poured it all into a water glass, wondering as she did if she might be doing her friend more harm than good. They did say whiskey was bad for snakebite, and if there ever was a snake, Ray Ellis qualified.

Mindy reached for the glass, saw that her hand was covered with blood, and, shuddering, drew it back, letting Kate hold the brandy to her lips. She coughed and her eyes teared, but in a moment she appeared stronger.

"Don't try to do it by yourself, Kate. Call the hospital."

Kate didn't want to tell her that they were cut off from help because she had been unable to find a radio. There was no way to call for the Mercy Bird.

She offered the alternative. "We'll take Ray's boat. It's big and fast. You could lie down and I know I can run it. We can get an ambulance in Simolona."

Blood, which she thought she had staunched with her layers of towels and strips of sheeting, oozed relentlessly through the sturdy fabric of Mindy's sweatshirt, spreading a scarlet stain over her chest.

Kate's eyes widened and she swallowed hard. It was too much, she knew that.

Mindy saw and smiled weakly. "No time, honey. Have to take the airplane."

Why did flyers always have to specify "air" plane? Kate wondered. Never just plane but always "air" plane.

"Phil's airplane," she said carefully. "But you can't fly it now and you know I can't! Ash?"

The old man, leaning on his crab net, shook his head.

"Cain't even drive no car," he said apologetically.

"Must try," said Mindy and slumped back on the chair with her eyes closed.

Panic seized Kate. "Fainted ... Ash, I think she's fainted! I don't remember what you do! ... cold water ... can't put her head between her knees. Smelling salts ... oh, dear God!"

"Fainting ain't so bad," offered Ash. "She don't feel the pain so horrendous that way. You git the car and I'll git the cold water. Be on the way in no time a-tall."

Kate stared at him. "On the way? You think I'm going to fly that plane?"

"Oh, ye with the fearful heart, be strong, fear not!" said Ash, adding gratuitously, "Jeremiah."

"Oh, you crazy old man!" Kate mumbled to herself and then added with a grin, "Mulcay." She ran down the back steps and climbed into Mindy's Jeep, driving it as close to the steps as the sand would permit. She left the motor running and the doors open while she ran into the house.

Ash was mopping at Mindy's forehead with a wet washrag, and she seemed to be sitting up a little straighter. Her eyes were open.

"I don't think you should try to walk," Kate said, eyeing the bloody front of the shirt.

"We gon' push her in the chair to the back door," said Ash, "and then betwixt us lift her as best we can into the ottymobile."

Mindy nodded and let them maneuver the chair toward the door, glancing back once to where Ray's body lay under the torn sheet. Her fine face with its sculpted planes sagged with grief.

Getting her into the Jeep was agonizingly slow. She tried to stand, and her knees buckled and she bit her lips to keep back a cry of pain. But the climb to the cockpit of the little Cessna was worse. With one on each side of her she helped to hoist herself up to the wing step and stood there a moment swaying.

If she falls, Kate thought, *it'll kill her.*

Mindy did not fall. She pulled herself erect and stepped into the cockpit, easing her body down to the right seat. Leaves me the pilot's seat, Kate realized with resignation.

Only then did she untie the ropes that secured the little plane to pins in the ground. Ash helped and was faster with them than Kate, whose fingers were dark with blood and fumbled clumsily.

When she climbed into the left seat, Mindy was struggling to fasten a seat belt and a shoulder harness, both of which were already stained with blood.

"Okay," said Kate, sliding under the wheel and reaching for the safety straps on her side. "You know I never flew an airplane in my entire life."

"Chocks," said Mindy faintly.

"What?" said Kate and then, "Oh, shoot, I forgot! At least I know that much!"

She leaned out the window and called to Ash. "Please move those chunks of wood from under the wheels!"

He gave her a lopsided salute and ducked under a wing. Emerging, he flapped an arm and surprisingly came out with a pilot's word: "Clear? All clear!"

"One more thing," she said, "stay here and wait for somebody to come. Don't go back to the house."

Kate looked at the array of knobs and switches in front of her in weary bafflement. Ash might as well have stayed his crab net and let Ray kill her. It would have been better than dying in the fiery crash she envisioned. Mindy, who had apparently been drowsing off, opened her eyes and said clearly: "Master switch ... left. Turn. Mixture control ... all the way in. Throttle ... push."

Kate couldn't read a word over any of those gadgets. She swiped at her glasses with her sleeve. Blood, already dried on them. Mindy's blood. She breathed on the lens and wiped them once more—this time on the knee of her jeans.

"Master switch ... turn," she repeated the instructions. She pawed at something that felt like a switch. "Mixture control ... this must be it ... all the way in. Throttle ... throttle?"

That must be the big knob where the gearshift was in her daddy's old Chevrolet, the one on which she had learned how to drive, except that one had been on the floor. She pushed.

"Key on left," said Mindy.

"Gotcha," said Kate. At least she knew a switch key when she saw it.

She turned it. The engine grunted and coughed and came to life.

"Now fly, damn you!" Kate cried. "Get on up there!"

The little airplane seemed to be trying to obey. It pulsed and palpitated, but it wasn't going anywhere.

"Go! Go!" Kate muttered, rocking back and forth in her seat as if that would propel it forward.

"Throttle," said Mindy, opening her eyes.

Kate reached for that fat gearshift-shaped knob and pulled and pushed. The push must have done it. The engine roared, the plane moved. In fact, it seemed headed for the weedy ditch at the edge of the field.

"Throttle back," said Mindy. "Put your feet on the rudders."

Kate looked at her sneakers and looked at what was in front of them. "You mean these pedal things?"

Mindy had lost interest and Kate, stiff with fear, experimented. They seemed to be directing the plane. She tried pushing in with her left foot and the plane turned left. She tried the right foot and the plane headed back for the ditch.

"Oh, Lordy," she moaned. But they had progressed as far as the runway and she knew enough from flying with other people to believe that the wind would be from the north-northwest in January. A good thing, if true, because she could never remember which end of that flabby wind sock hanging on the pole at the edge of the field represented the direction she needed. Little end or big end? It didn't matter; she had already turned north and she sure didn't know how to back up and turn around!

In the middle of the grass runway the plane picked up speed and Mindy reached for the throttle.

"I got it," said Kate, and she pushed.

Wonder of wonders, the plane lifted just in time to clear the scrub pine and sand dunes at the end of the runway.

"Thank you, thank you, God," Kate breathed. The wings waggled a little and Mindy pointed to the misshapen steering wheel. It was neither the joystick she read of in her stories of aviation pioneering nor a properly shaped steering wheel but something close—sort of flat on the top.

She held on to it.

Mindy gave a little sigh and slumped down, her head on her chest.

Oh, she's fainted again or she's dead! Kate told herself. They were over the water and the little plane seemed bent on taking a dip. It lunged forward and lifted a little, then bobbed toward the water and lifted again like a porpoise rising and plunging in the deep water. Kate clung to the wheel and searched the dash for a radio. There was one that only functioned when you were airborne, she had always been told. Did this porpoise-like plunging and lifting constitute being airborne?

She looked frantically for the radio and then saw the little round gray microphone, which the antic movements of the plane had dislodged and left dangling.

She grabbed it and her thumb found a button on its side.

"Is anybody out there?" she yelled. "Anybody at all? Answer me, somebody, please!"

It seemed eons before the box crackled a little and a voice said, "This is Tallahassee tower. You're on emergency frequency 121.5. Do you have a problem?"

"A PROBLEM!" screeched Kate. "I'm flying a plane and I DON'T KNOW HOW! I've got a dy ..." She looked at Mindy. "I've got a badly wounded woman bleeding and unconscious right here beside me! What am I going to do?"

Her voice broke and she felt desperate tears rising in her throat.

"Don't worry," said the faraway voice. "We'll get you in. My name is Rock and I used to be a flying instructor. What's your name? Do you know your position?"

"Kate Mulcay," she said promptly. That much was easy, but position ... position? Did he want longitude and latitude? She sure didn't know that. She had to tell that calm voice something.

"I just left Ila Island," she whimpered. "Headed north, I think."

"And you're not a pilot, Kate?" asked the voice.

"NO!" cried Kate. "I'm not a pilot!"

"That's all right," the voice soothed her. "It's not hard. I've always heard you can teach anybody to fly in an hour. Let's see what we can do in 20 minutes. That's about how far you are away. We'll get you in. Can you keep your airplane level?"

"I reckon so," said Kate. "It's been galumphing like a porpoise but it's better now."

"Push the throttle all the way in. Take your feet off the rudders," said the voice. "Pull back on the steering wheel. Do you see a compass? Look on the windshield above the panel."

Kate looked. She'd hated compasses since Girl Scout days when she got lost in the woods and the almighty compass failed to get her out.

"I see it, I guess," she said grudgingly.

"What does your compass say, Kate?" the voice asked inexorably.

Kate looked to Mindy for help, but she seemed totally out now. She took off her glasses and squinted at the little circle of glass on the windshield. "I see ten," she said.

"One zero," said Rock. "Okay, you are headed north. Continue on that heading and we'll pick you up on radar. Keep talking."

Keep talking, he says, Kate thought bitterly, like being nice at a cocktail party. What about?

"Mindy," she latched onto her friend's name. "Mindy is pretty bloody and she was in a lot of pain. I think she's unconscious again or ..." she gulped. "Or dead."

"Don't worry," said Rock. "You fly the airplane, Kate. We'll have an ambulance here for your friend. And emergency equipment ..."

That means a fire truck, Kate thought. He didn't want to suggest that we'll be coming down in flames.

"I have you on radar, Kate," the voice said, and suddenly Kate heard comfort in it. He wasn't an impersonal mechanical man. He was her best friend, her mentor, her savior. Even his name—Rock—promised that he was strong enough to get her out of this insane dilemma.

"What does your compass say now?" he asked.

Kate peered at it. "Zero," she said.

"Turn the airplane to the right until I say 'Stop,'" her new friend directed.

Kate turned the wheel a little and the voice said "Stop. Turn." And then, "Try to remain on your compass and if you do you'll be headed directly for the Tallahassee airport."

Kate peered out the left window. The sun was still high enough to flood the earth with golden light and to strike sparks where there were tin roofs on the little boxy houses. Fields and pine forests she knew well from ground travel seemed flat and unreal.

"What is your airspeed?" the radio asked

"I don't know!" wailed Kate. "I think we're standing still."

"Seems slow up there," said Rock, "but you're coming in pretty fast. Look at the gauge. How many RPMs does it show?"

Kate swallowed hard and tried to focus on the dials. Her hands on the wheel were damp. A lock of blood-stiffened hair pricked at her eyes. She pushed it back.

"I see a number," she said faintly. "It looks like 2,400."

"Take hold of that red knob," said Rock, "and pull it back until it hits 2,100."

Kate obeyed and waited for the little plane to ease

into a slow jog. Suddenly Mindy stirred. She was shivering and moaning.

The cheek toward Kate was smeared with blood she hadn't seen there before. Was she bleeding from the mouth or the nose? Kate leaned toward her and touched her forehead. It was icy. The cabin felt warm to Kate. Mindy was going to die of shock if not from bullet wounds, Kate thought frantically. She searched the luggage space back of the seats for a blanket or even a towel. Finding none, she started pulling off her own sweater with one hand, holding onto the steering wheel with the other.

It wasn't enough. The plane went crazy, swerving to the right like it might tip them out, nose up, heading for the sky. A funny humming noise sounded somewhere under the cowling.

"Rock!" she cried.

"What's happening?" Rock's voice was easy, devoid of alarm.

"I don't know!" Kate babbled. "Mindy's ... I think she's in shock. Cold. I was trying to ..."

"You pulled back on the wheel," Rock said. "Push it forward. Now ..." he said, watching the plane right itself on radar.

"There's a funny noise—a thrumming. Was. I think it's stopped now."

"You started a stall," Rock said. "That noise was a stall warning."

With one arm half in, half out of the sweater, Kate grasped the wheel and pushed at it until the plane seemed level. The humming noise had ceased. Stall, she thought. That had to be bad. If a car stalled it stopped. If an airplane stalled it must just drop out of the sky. She shivered.

Mindy opened her eyes and whispered, "Stall," and closed them again.

Where were you when I needed you? Kate mumbled crossly. A Ninety-Niner, one of Jacqueline Cochran's famous flying girls, out of commission—and here I am, a know-nothing police reporter, about to kill us. But that wasn't true. Hadn't she pushed the plane out of the threatened stall? A small tremor like self-confidence stirred within her and she let her eyes wander to the graying sky above her, the green and gold earth below.

The worst test of all lay ahead. Landing. The Talla-hassee airport seemed small and country-tranquil by comparison with Atlanta's Hartsfield, but still airliners landed there. Small planes came and went. Some-times—she gulped—planes crashed in midair. She had covered such a disaster once.

"Rock," she said timidly. "Will there be other planes when ..."

"When you land," Rock finished for her. "Don't worry about it. We'll clear your airspace. Now look out and tell me what you see. Do you see a lake, a water tank, a television tower?"

"No, no, none of that!" Kate cried. "Just trees and lit-tle bitty houses. Where's Tallahassee? Where's the sky-line?"

"Don't worry," said Rock. "When you're five miles

out you will see the airport. And at the end of the big runway you're going to take you'll see the numbers, a big 36. Watch for that. Tell me when you see it."

"I think I see it," Kate said worriedly after a moment.

"Okay," said Rock. "Stay off the radio now and listen to me. I'm going to talk you in. Ease back on the throttle to 1,800 RPMs. The plane has started descending. Push the wheel forward gently when I tell you to."

Kate listened so hard her ears hurt.

"Next to the throttle," said Rock, "is a little knob that says 'carburetor heat.' Pull it out all the way. Your engine is slowing down. You should be at 1,500 RPMs." Kate checked and it was so.

"When I tell you, start pulling back on the wheel very slowly. Now! Pull it back to your chest. Easy, easy. You won't be able to see over the nose but that's okay."

The ground was coming up to meet her. The plane, which had seemed to slow to a standstill in the air, was rushing hell-for-leather over the runway, heading, Kate was sure, for a bunch of steel-gray buildings beyond. She started to cry out to Rock, but he was talking.

"Hold it! Hold it!" he said. "You're running out of speed. The nose will gently fall forward and your wheels will hit the ground. You're doing fine, fine. Don't try to brake her. Let her roll to a stop."

The plane wobbled and headed for the grass field at the edge of the runway, but it stopped. Kate's instinct was to tromp on the brakes as she would in a car, but now she seemed conditioned to obeying Rock. She sagged in the seat, her arms limp at her sides.

The airplane suddenly seemed surrounded. An ambulance pulled up on the right side and two young men leaped out with a stretcher. A mechanic was tugging at Kate's door and grinning at her.

"You did it!" he cried. He offered her his hand and when she stood on the step he said, "Watch it! Don't fall! I got you!"

He was just in time. She found her eyes blurring and her body weaving drunkenly. Strong young hands half-lifted her to the concrete runway.

"I'm sorry," she murmured. "I seem to have run out of steam."

"Sure," said the young mechanic. "That wasn't easy, what you did."

"Where's Rock?" Kate asked, looking at the crowd gathering around her. "I want to thank Rock."

"He'll be out in a little while. He's about to go off-duty. Had a big plane coming in from Atlanta."

"Oh, I'd better not wait," said Kate, watching the stretcher with Mindy on it going into the ambulance. "I better go with her."

"Right," said the mechanic. "We'll take care of your airplane. Have it ready for you when you want to go back."

"Never mind!" said Kate emphatically. "I'll go back—IF I go back—by oxcart!"

She hurried to climb in the ambulance, but before the doors closed a pudgy middle-aged man with a bald head and the face of an anxious baby hurried up.

"I'm Rock!" he said, sticking out his hand. "Congratulations, Kate. You did great."

"I did?" Kate cried. "You did and I want to thank you. I ..."

But he had slammed the door and the ambulance was moving.

A hero, Kate thought, but he sure doesn't look like one. I don't know why I expected John Wayne or Gregory Peck.

At the hospital people in white uniforms took charge of Mindy and were wheeling her off to the emergency room when she came to and said faintly, "Kate, Nora's money—I borrowed it from Phil for Ray. I'll give it back."

She closed her eyes again and a black man with a kind face found Kate a chair in a quiet corner and brought her a cup of coffee.

"Don't you worry," he said soothingly. "We'll keep you posted on her condition."

Presently the outside doors opened and Greg Herren and Nora rushed in. In a matter of moments they were joined by a swarm of other islanders. Until the Winklers got there, nobody said anything much. Ash had told them enough about the double shooting and Kate's ignorant and inept making like a *Mercy Bird* to render them speechless for awhile. But the arrival of Deb and Dab and Winkie set off a babble of cries and birdlike cooings and bubbling prognostications and predictions, causing Nora to draw into a shell of silence, stiffly clutching the plastic arms of the hospital chair. Greg got up and paced the hall, and after a moment Kate went to join him.

"I'm sorry I didn't get back in time to avert that ... confrontation," he said after a time. "I suspected some of that, but I needed to check some things. While I checked, he shot Mindy. It could have been you and even Ash."

Kate looked at him curiously. For a new visitor to the island, he was taking a heavy role in its affairs. Why?

Greg sensed her question. "I'm with the Coastal Casino Control Commission," he said. "My bosses knew about the plans of Ray Ellis and his group and asked me to investigate. When they involved that pair from New York, we knew the deal smelled."

"You mean Count Alexis Bulgay and Henry Clay Somebody?"

Greg smiled for the first time.

"The Count," he said, "is a Brooklyn waiter. They call him 'Count' as a joke. He really can't count. You know what a counter is?"

Kate shook her head.

"Casinos aren't crazy about them. They are people with the uncanny talent of knowing and remembering every card that's played, especially in blackjack. The house hates it and bans the counters when it can. Bulgay has been kicked out of casinos here and there and he claims that it's because he's a counter. He's not that smart, but I guess he convinced Ellis. And Shenstone—Henry Clay, to you—is a small-time thug and gambler, the Count's sidekick."

"They beat up Ash and threatened to burn his house," Kate said.

"Ellis," said Herren. "He had some kind of morbid

notion that a cleared island, especially one without a lot of troublemaking conservation nuts, would attract big money. Also he might have known that Ash had seen the Langhorne girl killed and had acted to keep you from the same fate."

"Finley Sawyer and Paul Lewis?" Kate said.

"Finley was an asthmatic, allergic to many things. Somebody poison-sprayed his house for him. We can't prove that Ray set it up, but I think he did. Lewis was a dried-out alcoholic and a highly litigious lawyer who would never have quit until he found a court to stop development on the island. It's too late now to try to prove that Ellis and his friends kidnapped him and poured liquor down his throat in sufficient amounts to kill him. But I believe that's what happened. The sheriff is looking into it as a way of getting rid of the Count and Henry Clay."

"The Pinsons?" Kate asked.

Greg grinned. "You take it from here. I've about wound up my business on Ila. Or maybe I should say you've wound it up for me. I'll stay, of course, until we know how bad it is with Mindy. But I should be going home at the end of the week. Maybe I'll return someday."

11

▶Mindy was going to live. A young doctor came out and told them so. The bullet had entered her chest, grazed a rib, and lodged in her shoulder, missing all the vital organs. She had lost too much blood and suffered from shock, but they could handle that and she would probably be able to see her friends tomorrow.

"Mighty strong and resilient for a woman of her age," the doctor concluded, tucking his pen in his clipboard and closing it.

Kate looked at Nora and they laughed together. There would be another shooting if Mindy heard that horrid compliment—"a woman of her age."

Kate walked up the island to say good-bye to Ash before she went home. The afternoon was warm and the sound was as calm and green as picnic lemonade. Pepper raced ahead, hoping to terrorize as many shorebirds as would wait until the last minute to take flight in their leisurely decorous way.

She detoured past the shell mound, which looked peaceful in the late-afternoon light, and paused a moment to think about little Sarah Langhorne. There would be no reason to disturb her bones now to prove corpus delecti against a murderer.

Rest in peace, child, Kate whispered, laying a hand on the warm shell wall.

Ash was caught up in a frenzy of housekeeping. He had swept the sand in front of his door, tipped the rainwater out of the salvaged sail which shaded the walk to his privy, and was scrubbing his coffeepot.

"Hidy-do, Kate!" he called cordially. "Come, set. We'll have coffee out of a *clean* pot for a change."

"Might not taste as good," Kate said, and the old man guffawed appreciatively. The cut on his cheek had lost its bandage, but it seemed to be healing anyhow.

"I've got to get back to work, Ash," Kate said. "But I wanted to thank you for that dido you cut with the crab net. If you hadn't distracted him and thrown him off balance ... well, it probably would have killed me and maybe Mindy, too. You've been a good friend and ... oh, well, I'll be seeing you."

"You mought, more'n you think," Ash said. "I been ast to run the ferry. Temporary till they can git somebody to take hit reg'lar. You know I don't want to be reg'lar. But temporary ..."

"That's wonderful, Ash! You'll do a terrific job. You know the sound waters and all the sandbars better than anybody, and boats, too, although it is a powerboat and you'd prefer to use oars, now, wouldn't you?"

Ash grinned. "Likely I can run that ferryboat engine as good as you run that airplane," he teased.

"Touché!" said Kate, laughing and getting to her feet. "But I did get her there, didn't I?"

"You done good, Kate. I was jes' joreeing you. And if I do run the ferry, come back and I'll give you the cut rate."

"Thank you and bless you, *Captain!*" Kate said, waving and walking away.

The sun was close to setting when she got back to the sound beach, and she walked slowly to savor the last of its color before she had to leave for Atlanta.

The tide was going out, leaving a ruffled ribbon of sand which caught and held rosy light from the sky. Kate was only a random now-and-then collector of seashells, but her eye fell on an argonauta trapped in one of the ruffles on the flat. It was a rare shell in Ila waters and she stooped to pick it up. Delicately fluted and almost transparent, it was said to have been named for the ship that Jason sailed in search of the golden fleece. Kate held it gently, remembering the legend: a sign of fair weather and favorable winds. She carefully put it back in the sand at the edge of the surf.